Missives of Wisdom from an Inmate

Missives of Wisdom from an Inmate

ANA SILVIA CONTRERAS

ISBN-13: **9781533454614**
ISBN-10: **1533454612**
Library of Congress Control Number: 2016909550
CreateSpace Independent Publishing Platform
North Charleston, South Carolina

This book is dedicated to all cancer victims, survivors, and their families, and to all inmates in the prison system who have gained wisdom and have true repentance in their hearts, especially Jose Lazaro Contreras. Jose Lazaro, your missives have been my greatest inspiration, your words and wisdom have reminded me of what really matters in life, and your great sense of humor has made my heart and my soul smile. With my love, I thank you!

Foreword

We all have stories to tell. The simple fact that we are born is a story. Everyone's story is different. Some stories are happy, sad, funny, tragic, adventurous or exciting. Somehow, everyone has experienced some sort of joy, happiness, heartache or sadness in their life. We have all made mistakes, but that is life. Living teaches us lessons. We are human. Even if our parents gave us advice when we were young, we never really cared to listen. We kept making our own decisions and our own mistakes. Only after we had made those mistakes did we learn something from them. I am here to remind you that life can be hard, but it doesn't have to be.

Every day we make choices, and those choices will lead us to either good or bad results. Every action will have a reaction, good or bad. Life starts all over again each day when we wake up. With every new dawn, we have a new chance to start over. I am writing this book not to share my mistakes with you, but to share the great lessons I have learned during my life.

After living a life full of drama, conflict, and uncertainty, I have been able to learn from my mistakes. Since books were always my passion, and reading my comfort and escape, a few years ago I went back to reading books. This time, however, I chose my books carefully. I wanted to grow and learn, and I yearned for positive knowledge and wisdom. I no longer cared about romance or finding my Prince Charming, but wanted to find true joy and peace in my life. I wanted a healthy, balanced life: mentally, physically, and spiritually.

My greatest inspiration for this book is someone very close to me who I love very much. He is in prison serving a life sentence, and I have learned so much from him. Thanks to him, I now appreciate life more than I ever did before. He has been in prison for almost 18 years, and he is truly a smart, witty, charismatic, humble, noble, wise, articulate man and a great human being.

He has certainly opened my eyes and heart to the false stigma that inmates have to carry in prison and sometimes even after they are released. Society views them all with fear and rejection, but there are thousands of men and women in the prison system who have more integrity, respect, kindness, love and consideration for themselves and others than those who judged and sentenced them to prison, and even some of those who guard and protect them. There are inmates now serving life sentences who have acquired so much life wisdom that if given an opportunity, they would help improve our world. They would be better examples to follow than most of our politicians, religious leaders, law enforcement officers or other community leaders who have the power to create positive change and set good examples, but often do not. There are many inmates, however, who have committed heinous crimes and deserve to be in prison for many years, if not for life.

Society also tends to scrutinize and reject most people who have a criminal record. When they are released from prison, most of these men and women are in need of support and guidance, but instead find themselves being judged and rejected because they served time.

Most people will reject a person with a criminal record because they feel that they cannot trust them. This is wrong, because in most cases, people released from prison are looking for an opportunity to start a new life. They have paid their debt to society, yet society can be very unforgiving. Quite often, many of these men and women are not given a fair chance at a new life.

Employers tend to look down on them, and they often fall victim to employers and other people they encounter. They are being set up to fail, because often they cannot find work and have no means of support. They end up committing a crime to get money for food, and sadly, this leads to many of them ending up in prison again. Although they did commit a crime, not every inmate is a bad person. All they want is an opportunity to enjoy something we often take for granted: our freedom.

Many of these men and women will often tell you how most of us take life and all of our blessings for granted. The simple fact that you can get up right now and walk outside to enjoy the sunlight or moonlight, and feel the wind caress your skin, enjoying your freedom, is something that so many inmates will never have a chance to ever experience again.

Everyone makes mistakes, but some are paying so much more than others. This story is about being human and making mistakes, about love and family, and life's challenges, but most importantly, about having faith in God.

I want to tell everyone that it does not matter how low you have fallen. You can still get up. You can still gain control of your life and find the happiness that all of us have been seeking since we were small children. You can find inner peace and success in every aspect of your daily life. You can learn to find joy in giving, to love everyone, to forget wrongs and forgive everyone, which includes forgiving yourself.

I will take you on a journey of today's challenges and obstacles, and share with you how you can also gain control of your life. Every day you wake up should be better than the day before. I am here to help you understand the things in life that really matter.

I have made my share of mistakes, and I have fallen, managed to get up, and confronted my fears, my doubts, and my dreams. Nothing would make me happier in life than to learn that somehow my story has taught you everything you need to know to survive in today's chaotic world. I want it to inspire you to be the very best version of who you are truly meant to be.

I hope that you will enjoy everything I have to share, and that you will find value in my story and can share it with others to motivate them to get up and try again. You do have to ask yourself what it is that you want most. What is missing from your life right this moment? What are your goals and your dreams in life?

In order to achieve anything in life, you must have a great desire to accomplish that specific goal or dream. You must not allow anything to become an obstacle and prevent you from achieving your dreams. What is success to you? What are you doing to change the course of your life and your current circumstances?

Over the years, I have often heard people quote Einstein, saying that the definition of insanity is doing the same thing repeatedly but expecting different results. Consistency is so important in anything you may want to achieve. What are your dreams? You must first convince yourself that this is what you really want. Get up, and together let us help you get the results that you deserve. You were born to succeed; to thrive, and all you have to do is get back on course.

So many self-help books, videos, audios, conventions, and seminars teach you to believe in yourself. If you don't believe in yourself, you will never accomplish anything. You must first believe it, visualize it, then act it and become it. Everything in life starts with a thought, which becomes an action, then a habit, and eventually leads to your character.

Don't let anything or anyone prevent you from being happy, because you deserve happiness. The cruelty, heartache, shame, anger, hatred, and suffering that you endured or that you caused others is now in the past. It is gone. Don't let it control you; you can control it by not allowing it to enter your thoughts or consume your brain. Everyone is capable of improvement and change, but no one else can change you. Only you can do that.

I pray that this story will teach you about life and how to live it, and that you can teach others to live a life full of love, laughter, and emotional, physical, spiritual, and mental health.

One

He stared at his image in the mirror. His mother had told him that he had the kind of face that would make you stop and stare. He had swirling, dark brown hair that danced in the wind and bedazzling, tourmaline green eyes. They were round as opals and the pathway to his soul. He had bushy black eyebrows that were an artist's dream. His arched cheekbones appeared flushed as he stared at his image in the mirror. He had a rugged, masculine marble jaw and an imperial nose.

He was wearing a muscle shirt, and he could see his Atlas shoulders above a barrel chest. He had a gym-honed physique and iron-wrought muscles. He had just come back from running five miles, and the sensation of the water had been a blessing as he showered. The image in the mirror pleased him. He smiled, feeling a tingling warmth in his limbs and an expansion in his chest, and despite his circumstances, he felt great.

His mother had often told him that he looked dashing, with a roguish smile. The thought of his mom made him smile again. He grabbed the towel from the rack and dried his face, then put it back as he walked out of the bathroom into the kitchen.

It was Joel's 18th birthday, and he should have been ready to celebrate this very special day. He was now officially an adult, but although he was celebrating his birthday, there would be no room for a party, music, birthday cake or any kind of celebration with friends or loved ones. He felt that he had matured so much in the last year, with everything that had happened in his life.

He held his breath for an instant and exhaled, feeling a slight heartache as he suddenly remembered what he was still facing. He felt like he was moving in slow motion as soon as he saw the envelope resting on the kitchen table.

Joe walked with sure-footed purpose to the table and picked up the envelope that he was sure contained a birthday card. It was a plain white envelope with his name written on the front in red ink. He recognized his mother's beautiful feminine handwriting. Too bad he had not inherited her penmanship.

He glanced at the writing on the front of the envelope, which read, "Happy Birthday, Joel. I love you, Mom." He realized at that moment that he was crying. As the warm tears ran down his cheeks, he felt them burning his skin as if they were acid. He loved his mother so much. She had been and always would be the strongest, kindest person he had ever met. Life was not fair to her, because she was still battling breast cancer.

She had endured so much in the last year, and he knew that she would not be happy with him if she knew that he was crying or that he was worried about her. He wasn't crying because he was worried; his tears were tears of joy. He was grateful to God that his mother was still there with him to celebrate his birthday. Months earlier he had thought he was going to lose her, and had been afraid that she would not be with him to celebrate his next birthday. He closed his eyes for a few seconds, remembering the experience.

A year earlier, after visiting the doctor and then seeing a specialist, her diagnosis had been breast cancer stage 3C, which had spread beyond the breast and underarm area. The mammogram the doctor had ordered had confirmed the diagnosis. She did not want to tell Joel about her condition at first, but eventually she did.

His mother was a warrior, a fighter, and she was not about to give up on life without a battle. Because of the tumor's size, and since it had spread to three of the 15 lymph nodes they removed from her arm, they began chemotherapy to shrink it. She had several months of treatments, and recently what was hopefully her last surgery. Joel knew that his mother would win the battle against breast cancer, but it had been so hard for her.

She would always smile and say that she was doing fine, when Joel knew that she was really suffering. He didn't understand how his mother could be so strong and courageous. He just wanted to know that after all she was enduring, her doctor would tell her that she was cancer-free. He felt a willingness to believe that everything would be all right, and filled his mind with positive thoughts.

Each treatment had left her very fatigued, and she began to lose her hair. Although she had once had long, beautiful hair, she was not at all concerned about losing it. Vanity was the least of her worries. Shortly after she started losing her hair, she began wearing scarves to cover her head. She always smiled and did the impossible to appear as if she were winning her battle against cancer.

She told Joel that she knew that God would save her. She constantly reminded him that as long as her heart was still beating, she would never lose hope, and she needed him to do the same. At first, that had been very difficult for him, because he had feared where that new path in their life was going to lead them.

He thought of her in her bedroom, took a deep breath, and did what he always did. He made himself happy for her, even though his heart ached to see her suffering the way she was. He could not let her down and let her see his pain. He ran his hand through his hair and relaxed his muscles, feeling a lightness in his chest and a sense of calm.

He remembered something that Abraham Lincoln had said about happiness: "Folks are usually about as happy as they make their minds up to be. Every person's happiness is their own responsibility." As Joel thought about that quote, he remembered that it had been very hard for him to really believe at first. His mother had always preached and lived by that rule. He was doing the impossible to feel that way, but it had not been easy.

God knows, Joel wanted to be very happy, but how could he if the single most important person in his life was suffering so much and could still die? He felt so much older than 18, but he had not yet gained enough maturity to fully understand his mother's circumstances and why she was sick. She didn't deserve it. She deserved to live a long, happy, healthy life. She was a great mother and a wonderful human being.

Life had dealt her a bad hand. She had always worked so hard to provide for him, and had dedicated her life to loving and raising him. He had never met his father; or rather, he did not remember him. His mother told him that his father had left when Joel was six months old. He had no memories of his father and didn't care about him. He wasn't important to Joel.

He had only asked his mother about him once when he was seven years old, and she had told him that when the time was right, she would talk to him about his father. He never asked about him again. He wasn't sure why he was even thinking about him right at that moment, but how could he really think about him if he had no idea what he looked like?

He took another deep breath and opened his birthday card. He smiled when he saw the cute caricature of a little person on the front of the card holding a sign that read, "Smile while you still have teeth. Happy Birthday, Son," and couldn't help but laugh. His mother was so wonderful. She always reminded him that no matter how challenging things got, he always had to keep his sense of humor and laugh every day.

She always said that laughter was the remedy for any illness, and that Joel should always find something to laugh or smile about. She had always used humor to lighten any moment, and Joel had learned so much from her.

As he opened the card, he read about how much his mother loved him and her best wishes for his birthday and every day of his life. She would always include a birthday quote, and this year's quote read, "Happy Birthday, Joel. As you get older, always make sure that you don't count the years, but make the years count." The card didn't have any cash or gift cards, but to Joel, his mother's words were worth more than all the money in the world. His only wish had been and would continue to be that she would heal and get better.

He put the card back in the envelope, took a deep breath, and walked slowly toward his mother's bedroom. He stood outside the door for a couple of seconds before he took a deep breath and gently tapped on it. Then he heard her weak voice inviting him to come in.

He strode into the room with a big smile. He approached her bed and slowly sat on the edge as he leaned and kissed her gently on the cheek. She looked so fragile, but less ill. As always, she smiled at him. Her smile was magical; he could see that she was smiling from her heart. He gently rested his head on her legs, making sure not to apply any unnecessary pressure. She looked so much older than 38.

He could see strands of his mother's midnight black hair peeking out of the corner of the scarf she was wearing. A pair of arched eyebrows looked down on long eyelashes that had no need for mascara. Her delicate ears framed an elegant nose. She had enthralling green eyes and pouty lips. Despite her illness, her eyes had never lost their shine. Her once beautiful cheekbones and glossy skin looked pale and emaciated. But to Joel, his mother was still the most beautiful woman in the world.

Before his mother had gotten sick, people would often tell her that she was beautiful and that she looked like Sophia Loren. They thought she was much younger than her age. Many times when Joel and his mother were out together, people would assume that she was his sister, and there had been times where they thought he was her boyfriend. She would laugh at those comments. She would say, "What is this world coming to, Joel, when it's acceptable for older women to date men who could be their children, and society sees it as normal?"

"Do you know that they have a name for that, Mom? They call them cougars." His mother had remarked that people were truly losing their minds, and moved away from the subject. She felt it was a waste of time to talk about things of little importance to them.

"Happy Birthday, Joel. I'm so proud of you and the man that you have become. It seems like it was just yesterday that you were born and I was holding you so close to my heart." Her voice was soothing, and she spoke quietly as she gently stroked his hair with her right hand.

"Thank you, Mom. I can't believe that I'm 18 years old either, and thank you for the beautiful birthday card, and for my life and all the wonderful things you have done for me." He smiled broadly. He would never let her see him suffer for her. He loved her so much.

"Did you like the birthday card I bought you?" She forced a smile.

"I loved your card, Mom. It's very funny, and yes, I guess I should smile while I still have teeth." He smiled back at her as he opened his mouth to show her his teeth and make her laugh. "How do you do it, Mom?" he asked, looking at her tenderly.

"What do you mean, Joel?"

"Your spirit, your passion for life in spite of everything?" he asked in a deep voice.

"Well, first of all is my faith in God. I know that no matter what happens, God will make the best decision for me. I am no one to question anything; all I can do is do my best to beat the cancer, and the rest I leave up to God."

"Mom, I want so badly to be as brave as you are, to have that optimism that you have in spite of everything you've gone through in the last year. I wish I could have your faith."

"With time, you'll be more mature and have more understanding, son. You are such a brave young man; you have always been brave, Joel. I don't want you to fret over my condition. I've always taught you that we only focus on the things we can control, and beyond that, we leave everything to God."

"Yes, I do know that, Mom. I've always only focused on the things that I can control, but this has been really hard for me to understand or accept," he responded gently.

"Joel, remember when you were 13 and came to me and asked me why you were so different from all your friends?"

"Yes, of course I remember that conversation."

"I told you that you weren't different, but just very mature, and that you had learned a lot of things about life at 13 that most teenagers usually don't know, or rather, don't care to know. You have always been ahead of all your friends in your maturity level."

"I just always felt so different. Even now I still feel different from my friends."

"There's a reason why you're that way, son."

"Well of course there is, Mom. It's because you raised me that way, and honestly, I would never change that. I couldn't have asked for a better mother." He smiled at her.

"Joel, I have something really important that I have to share with you," she said, lifting his chin gently so that her bright green eyes were looking straight into his. "Can you please open the closet door for me and grab the brown shoebox that's on the top shelf?"

He gently released himself from her touch, walked over to the closet and opened it. On the top shelf, he saw the brown shoebox that his mother had described. He had seen that shoebox so many times over the years and had never thought anything of it.

He grabbed the box, which was resting on top of a stack of sweaters, and with trembling hands, turned around and faced his mother. The box wasn't very heavy, only a few pounds. He was sure it contained legal documents. Perhaps his mother was going to hand him his birth certificate and other documents that he might need in the future. Why were his hands trembling? What was really inside the box?

He looked so happy, just like he was supposed to. She should never know how much he really hurt. He had to be very strong for her, and he would make sure that she felt his support. He would never give her a reason to worry about him.

If only she knew that he was having a hard time accepting things as they were. He wanted to be as understanding as his mother was, but he hoped that with time he would acquire more of her wisdom. He really wished that he had her maturity, her strength.

"Here you go, Mom." He placed the box gently on top of her legs, instead of handing it to her, since he felt that she was too weak to hold it.

"I have something really important to share with you, Joel. I've been waiting until I felt the time was right for me to have this conversation with you. The time is now. Not only because I've been so sick, son, but also because now you're officially an adult. The contents of this box were meant to be given to you on your 18th birthday, and I just thank God that I'm still here to deliver this to you," she said as she cleared her throat.

"Of course you're still here, Mom, and you'll still be here with me for a long time. I have all the faith in God that you'll overcome this, but what does this shoebox have to do with anything?"

"When you were seven years old, you asked me about your father, and I told you that it wasn't time yet for you to learn about him. For some odd reason, you never asked about him again, which made things easier for me. I didn't have to try to give you the same excuse every time. I didn't want to have to lie to you." She moved the box to the side of the bed as she attempted to sit up straight.

"I have to tell you a story about your father before I give you the box. Joel, I'm praying that everything that I have taught you will stay with you and that you'll have the maturity to understand certain things, son. I'm praying that you won't pass judgement on your father and who he was."

Joel had questions in his mind and he needed answers. He was not going to pressure his mother into answering those questions. He would only take whatever she had to share with him. His heart was racing, and he felt as if it would burst out of his chest any second. He looked at his mother lying on the bed, his forehead creased with worry. The thought of his father filled his heart with an inexplicable emotion.

He had never understood why his mother had never dated or remarried. Somehow, he had always believed that his father was the reason, but he was never certain. She was very beautiful, and plenty of men had tried to court her, but she always turned them down. She would always say that the only man she needed and wanted in her life was Joel.

His mother began: "Your father was born into a very poor family. He had a lot of brothers and sisters, and they all had to work when they were young. His father, your grandfather, owned a small landscaping business, and he and his five brothers worked really hard to help his father. They would do anything their father asked of them. He had an older sister whom he adored, and she adored him.

From the time your father was a very young boy, he was an entrepreneur at heart and was always looking for ways to help his parents generate some income, despite how young he was. He worked so hard and always wanted to please his father. His sister loved him very much, and said that even when he was small, he always wanted to spread joy and make others feel good. He had a great sense of humor, and he was always very helpful and fearless about everything.

When he was 11 years old, he would take soda and candy to school and sell it to his schoolmates to help his parents make some money. Your dad was very charismatic and likeable. He made friends easily, and they would buy things from him. He was very trustworthy, and people were always ready to buy from him."

"He felt good about helping his parents out," she said. "His goal was always to find a way to make money to help his family." She went on eagerly. "He wanted to make his father proud and show him that he could help him make money to pay the bills." She closed her eyes and took a calm breath.

"Your grandfather was a very ambitious man. He soon realized that his son could do much more than sell soda and candy. He wanted power and money, so over time, he replaced the soda and candy that your dad was selling at school with marijuana. Thanks to your grandfather, your father started selling drugs at the age of 12." She was breathing hard as she spoke. It was as if she were fighting for air.

"Mom, are you okay? We don't have to talk about this right now. Get some rest; we can talk about it some other day." He said this because he worried so much about her and her condition. Even though she was supposed to be getting better since her last surgery, he wanted to make sure that she was all right.

"No, son. I'm fine; don't worry, we have to talk about this now." She took a deep breath and continued her story. "Your grandfather's dream came true, and with time, his entire family was dealing drugs for him. He was wealthy and powerful. Your grandfather truly believed that a man without money was not a real man, and that only money gave you power and respect. He believed that only money mattered in life if you wanted to call yourself a real man." She placed the pillow behind her back and straightened herself in bed before she continued speaking.

"They were at the peak of success in their business when I met your father. I fell in love with him, his personality, not knowing what he did for a living. He told me when he met me that he worked in the family business; I just had no clue that the family business was drug dealing. I would have never have gotten involved with him if I had known that."

"How did you meet my father?"

"I was working as a teller at a local bank and your father came into the bank to buy a cashier's check. When he walked up to my window and smiled at me, I knew then that my life would be changing forever."

"After I first met him, he kept coming to the bank every week. He would always wait for me to help him with his transactions. He was so friendly and handsome that I began to hope that I was the reason for his weekly visit to the bank, not any transaction."

"At first, he was just friendly and never said or did anything to show that he had any personal interest in me. As he stood in line at the bank, I could see how friendly he was with the other customers waiting in line, and just friendly in general with everyone. He gave extra attention to the older customers. He seemed very caring and respectful."

"Every time he came up to the teller window and looked at me, my heart melted, and I loved the sound of my name as he pronounced it. He would always say, "How is your day going today, Alexia?" He had a volcanic voice, loaded with stamina. His smile was so captivating, just like yours."

"I had ended my shift one Friday evening, and when I walked out to my car, I saw him standing next to a black BMW smiling at me. For a second, I wasn't sure what to do, but he took matters into his own hands as he walked up to me and greeted me by my name. He really enjoyed saying my name for some reason."

"He told me that he really liked me and wanted to get to know me a little better, and that if his wanting to get know me personally created a conflict of interest because I worked for the bank, than he would just have to close his accounts and change banks."

"He asked me out for dinner that night and I said yes. It was one of the most special nights of my life. He was so charming, funny and very intelligent. He could talk about anything and everything, and he was so likeable with anyone that encountered him, even a total stranger. I stayed out with him talking while we had coffee after dinner. They had to ask us to leave because they were closing the restaurant."

"I don't know if he did it on purpose or not, but as we were getting into his car, he turned on the radio and the song "Drive" was playing. He looked at me and turned up the volume as he winked at me. I will never forget that song, and every time I listen to it, it takes me back to that moment and how he made me feel."

"A couple of months later, I had gone on several dates with him, and then he asked me to be his girlfriend. He was so adorable and charismatic that I fell for him right away and accepted him as my new boyfriend."

"Did you meet his family?"

"I met your father's family just before we were married. He did the impossible to keep me from meeting his family, especially his father. He has one sister and five brothers."

"So I have a big family, Mom?"

"Yes, you have a really big family, son. I married your father only six months after I met him, and then you were born. By the time you were born, your father opened up to me, confided in me, and told me about the family business. I couldn't believe what he was telling me, but when it finally sank in, I refused to be part of any of it, and at first I was upset with your father for being dishonest with me. I felt deceived, but I really loved him."

"I asked him to leave everything for us, or I would leave and take you with me, and he was willing to do it. He was in the process of leaving everything. He had already made up his mind. We had already planned where we would move and what we do, and we were both very excited about our future together with you. Neither of us were concerned about money; we only wanted to be together as a family."

"It seems that the DEA and FBI had been following your dad and his family for a while, and they had tapped their phones and were listening in on their conversations. It was only a matter of time before they arrested him."

"You were only six months old when he was arrested, but I want you to know that you were his pride and joy, and he loved you so much, but he got caught before we could get away from that lifestyle and start a new life."

"The day that they arrested him, we had an argument, because when I met him he smoked, and I really didn't like it. He told me that he only smoked socially, and he rarely smoked while I was around. He had made an effort to quit smoking for him and for us."

"That morning I got out of the shower, and he had you in bed playing with him. I could hear your giggles in the bathroom, but when I walked into the bedroom, you were lying on his stomach smiling and giggling and your dad was holding you with his left hand, resting his head against a pillow, and he was holding a cigarette in his right hand. He was staring out the window, looking really lost in thought."

"I was so upset with him for smoking around you. I told him to make sure he never did that again, and that if he wanted to smoke, he should do it when we weren't around. I didn't even stop and ask myself why he was smoking around you. Unfortunately, son, that image of your father lying in bed with you smiling and giggling and him holding a cigarette plays over and over in my mind."

"I really believe that your father may have known what was about to happen, because he truly only smoked when he was upset about something or if we were out at a social event. I wish that I hadn't been so upset with him, but I was only looking out for you and for him."

She gave Joel a few moments to absorb what she had just told him. Joel kept quiet, attentively waiting for her to keep speaking. He had a glazed look in his eyes.

"When we started planning our new life away from everything, I made it really clear to your father that his money didn't mean anything to me, that leading an honest life where we could raise you with the right morals, integrity and principles was far more important to me, but we didn't get a chance to leave. We weren't going to take much of anything. That day was the last day I saw your father as a free man. He was arrested only a few hours later."

"Is he still in prison, Mom?"

"Yes he is, son. Your father was given a life sentence," she said quietly.

"What did he really do to get a life sentence?" Joel asked as he cocked his head.

"It's not so much what he did, it's more what he didn't do that got him a life sentence."

"I don't understand, Mom. What was it that he didn't do?"

"Your father could have very well have served 8 to 10 years in prison for the charges they had on him, but because he didn't turn in everyone else that was involved, especially not his father, he pretty much took the blame for everyone, never realizing that he was going to be given a life sentence. He was charged as the "leader organizer." Your father never in a million years imagined that his sentence would be that harsh."

Joel was speechless as he heard his mother tell him their story. He felt so confused and wanted to say so much, but he knew that he would never say anything that would hurt his mother any more than she had been hurt all her life. He did not interrupt her. His poor mother had suffered enough.

"You see, son, after he was sentenced, when I went to visit him in prison he made me promise him that I would never talk to you about him until you were an adult. He didn't want the shadow of having a father as a criminal in your life creating obstacles or self-doubts about how wonderful you were and would be."

"He also forbade me from ever visiting him. Your father was 28 years old when he received his sentence. The only thing that he said to me was that he loved me too much to keep me from moving on with my life, and he wanted me to be happy." The tears ran down her cheeks. "I loved your father then, and I love him now, and will love him until my last breath," she said. Her right hand pressed against her breastbone as she let out a whimper.

"Mom, please don't cry. I don't want you getting upset. You're not well; you have to save your strength. Please, Mom, I can't bear to see you upset. You're the most wonderful mother in the whole world; you were my mother and father all of these years, and I'll always be grateful for that. I don't want to see you suffer, it kills me to see you this way," Joel said as he gently rubbed her back.

"I'm fine, son. I'm not really crying for myself, Joel. I'm crying for your father. I feel like your father was a good man, a kind man who missed an opportunity to have a decent life. I know that he made a conscious decision to stay in his father's business once he was an adult and he should pay for that, but he shouldn't have taken the blame for everyone else and gotten a life sentence." Her voice was shaky.

"Mom, you've always told me that every action has a reaction, good or bad. My father is paying for his wrong actions. He made a choice, and this is the result of his choice. I understand that he didn't want me to be in his life because he was in prison, but somehow, knowing myself and being raised the way you raised me, I don't think that would have kept me from becoming the man I am and will be."

"I tried convincing him that we needed to be part of his life and that he needed to be part of ours regardless of the situation, but he wouldn't give in. He made me swear and promise that I would pretend that he had died, and that I would make every effort to be happy with you," she said gently.

"I had somehow accepted his request, but a few weeks before your first birthday he called me and asked me to come visit him in prison. You have no idea how happy I was to hear from him, and when I went to see him, I couldn't wait to see him, to hear his voice. I knew then that I would always love him, that there would be no one else in my life. I could also see in your father's eyes that he truly loved me and that he was suffering for us and for him. It killed me to see him behind bars and to be able to speak with him only through a window. I wanted so badly to hold him and be held, and knowing and understanding that that would never happen was very painful."

"He told me that he had given a lot of thought to what our lives would be like without him there for us, and although he and I had only known each other for less than two years, he knew that we had so much in common. He really believed that if he had had an opportunity to walk away from his life, he and I would have had a wonderful healthy family."

"I have to tell you that I believed him. Your father asked me to let him help me raise you as if he had been part of your life. He said that he had decided that even though he was going to be in prison, he wanted to be part of your upbringing. He wanted to raise you. You may not believe this, son, but your dad was a good man."

"How can you say that he was a good man, Mom?"

"Because he really was. He wasn't given a fair chance at life, that's all. He told me that he took full responsibility for his actions and for being in prison, but that his sentence was unfair, and also how they had labeled him the leader organizer."

"He said he had thought long and hard about his absence and your upbringing, and he wanted to make a proposal that would benefit you, him, and me. At first, I wasn't sure how that was going to be possible, but he asked me to give him a chance to explain what he wanted to do."

"He told me that every year on your birthday he was going to mail two letters to me. One would be for me to read, and the other one would be for me to save for you."

"I don't understand what you're saying, Mom." Joel said.

"Your father sent me a message each year for your birthday, and each message contained a principle, a law that would allow you to learn and understand each principle, and I would teach you to master it. Each principle was there to teach you, to mold you, until with time each principle would develop into a habit. Once each principle became a habit, it would shape your character, which would help you lead a successful mental, emotional, physical, and spiritual life."

"He said that if he had not been in prison, that is exactly how he intended to raise you."

"I'm trying to understand what you're saying, Mom," Joel said gently, tilting his head and pursing his lips.

"The principles were meant to teach you how to live a life of integrity, and to help build a foundation that would mold you into a noble, strong, kind, humble, hardworking, smart man. Each principle was meant for me to understand and focus on, then master it and teach it to you throughout each year. During your upbringing, every year when I received a new message, I was to learn something new and teach it to you, while still carrying over the lessons from the principle for the previous year."

"I can't believe what I'm hearing, Mom. All these years, I thought my father had just abandoned us. Never in a million years would I have believed what you just shared with me."

"Joel, please know that your father loved you from the moment you were conceived, and I know that he will love you until his last breath. He made a huge mistake in life and he has paid for that. When your father sent me the letters each year, I don't think he ever realized that I would also be learning and growing at the same time. Those letters have kept me strong and have helped me more than you will ever imagine. I don't think I would have become the woman I am without your father's letters."

"Mom, I'm just confused about everything you just shared with me. I'm sorry, but it's going to take a little while for me to understand all of this," he said, rubbing his forehead.

"I know, Joel. Inside the shoebox, you'll find every letter that your father sent to you for each of your birthdays. The last letter came in the mail yesterday. Take your time and read them whenever you like. After that, you and I will talk, and I'll answer any questions you may have," she said gently.

When Joel picked up the box, it suddenly felt very heavy, but he knew it was his imagination. He felt mentally numb and wanted to be alone and think things through. His legs felt weak, and he felt a sudden need to sit down, losing his balance for a moment. He almost dropped the box, but managed to grab it with both hands, pressing it against his chest. He could not believe what his mother had just shared with him.

"Joel, I don't want you to be upset about this. I know that I probably should have opened up to you and told you the truth sooner, but I also wanted to respect your father's only wish. This secret has been weighing heavily on my heart for so long, and I just wish that things could have been different for all of us. I hope you're not upset with me, son."

"I would never be upset with you. I love you too much for that. This is just a lot for me to take in. I can't tell you that it hasn't confused me, because then I would be lying to you, and that's something we don't do," he said, narrowing his eyes.

"Things will be fine, Joel. Your father has been mailing these letters every year, and I know that although he last saw you when you were six months old, he loves you with all his heart and only wants the best for you."

"I'd really like to believe that, Mom. Please don't worry too much about me. I'll be fine," he said uncertainly.

"Great, son. Smile and be happy, because you have so much to be grateful for. Your life is full of blessings," she said, taking a deep breath.

"I'm happy just being here with you. Having you in my life is my greatest blessing, and nothing makes me happier than hoping that soon you'll be healed and we'll look forward to a brighter future for all us."

"I have all the faith in God that I'll beat the cancer. I know that what I just shared with you was too much for you. I want you to know, Joel, that I can answer any questions you may have. Do you know that we only did what we thought was best for you?"

"I do believe that, Mom. I'm sure that I can speak with you freely and ask you any questions I may have," he responded slowly.

"Joel, I know that you should be out having a great time with your friends, celebrating your birthday, not here at home with me, but it was you who decided to stay home, so I decided to give you your father's letters today. You can read them today or whenever you want. It took your father years to write them, so you can take your time reading them."

"Thanks, Mom. Don't worry about me or that I didn't go out with my friends to celebrate my birthday. I couldn't think of anyone else to share my birthday with that would be more special to me than you. I love being with you, being around you."

"I'm sorry I didn't get you a cake, son. I almost had the strength to get up and bake you one, but my body betrayed me, and besides, baking was never one of my talents." She forced a smile.

"Mom, it's okay. I love you so much, and the only thing that matters to me is that you're here with me, and that you do the impossible to get better." He gave her a big smile and winked at her, feeling determined not to let his immediate emotions take control of his mind. He suddenly became aware of his own heartbeat and a sudden shiver that brought him pleasure.

"You are such a handsome young man, just like your father. Inside the box, you'll also find a picture of your father. Read his letters, son, and I hope that you'll be able to find all of the answers that I know are in your mind right now. Those letters will be like finding the missing puzzle pieces to complete your life." She touched his cheek and smiled at him.

"It may sound strange for me to say this to you again, son, but your father was a good man who had a bad upbringing, bad influences in his life, and a horrible foundation. I really believe that if your father had had a different upbringing he would have been a great man."

"Don't worry, Mom. I'll read them, but the most important thing for me right now is you. You have to take care of yourself and not do or say anything that will upset you."

"Go on, son. I'm fine, and you'll be next door. If I really need you, I'll just call you. I love you, Joel." She leaned forward and placed a gentle kiss on his right cheek. Happy birthday, Joel, and I know that right now, maybe nothing makes sense, but it will soon. You'll see once you read the letters."

Joel gently kissed his mother on the forehead as he walked out of the bedroom carrying the box that could change his life forever.

He now understood some things in his life that had sometimes not made much sense as he was growing up. He felt sad to know that his father was alive and had been in prison since he was a baby, but he had so many questions that his mother had not yet answered.

Perhaps she was right, and once he read his father's letters he would find the answers that he was so desperately searching for. Carrying the box with both hands, he walked toward his bedroom, anxious to open it and read its contents.

His heart was heavy as he walked away from his mother's room. He realized how much his mother had suffered all her life. His father was alive, and now he knew that his mother had never remarried because of her feelings for his father. She had just confirmed that.

With large strides, he headed toward his bedroom. He was now officially an adult, and he had to behave like one and face whatever life was going to throw his way. This was yet another life test, and he was going to make sure that he passed it and walked away with newfound wisdom.

It was his birthday, and he intended to be thankful to God for everything in his life. He decided that learning that his father was alive was the best birthday present he could have wished for.

He remembered that on his seventh birthday he had blown out the candles and made a wish; he had wished for his father to be in his life. He smiled at the idea of all of the changes that he felt he would soon experience. Who needed cake and a party when you could get the father you had only dreamt of having?

Despite his confusion, Joel smiled with the knowledge that his father had loved him and that he had always been in his mind and heart. He had a feeling that it would be a very happy birthday indeed.

Two

*H*e opened the door to his bedroom and went in. He laid the shoebox on the bed, closed his eyes and slowly opened it, feeling many different emotions. He took a deep breath before opening his eyes and reaching inside the box. His father's picture was right on top, and appeared to have been there for a long time. His eyes wide, he stared at the picture, raising his eyebrows as his lips parted. He shook his head in disbelief. His mother was right. He looked just like him; the resemblance was remarkable. He grabbed the picture and stared at it, as if he were trying to communicate with his father through the picture, then slowly laid it on the bed.

He wondered what else he had inherited from his father, besides his looks. What kind of man was his father? He knew that his mother really believed that he could have been a great man, but she had known him for such a short time that she could be wrong. Also, anyone in their right mind would disagree with her, saying that men in prison are never great, but rather a disgrace to society.

Now he understood why his mother had never dated anyone. She had dedicated her life to raising and loving him. He had always suspected that his father was the reason why his mother never went out with any men, and now he knew he had been right.

He thought about his upbringing, and at first, he never would have suspected anything, but now he remembered how his mother used to become more enthusiastic around his birthday. She always made it fun and exciting. He had not realized it then, but thinking back, Joel could see how his mother always said or did something that reminded him of his previous birthdays. He felt like he had always learned something new on his birthday.

He had always felt like he was much more mature than most of his friends. He had always been the one to keep them all out of trouble by having a sense of maturity that had seemed normal to him, but not to his friends.

If he really wanted to, he could go back through the last nine or 10 years and remember what his mother had taught him about life. He was sure that once he read his father's letters he would read about all of the things he already knew. He would remember all of his mother's teachings.

His upbringing would not allow him to judge anyone like his father, but he never would have believed that someone in prison could share wisdom or good advice about life. Their environment was difficult, sad, and horrific. Inmates lived in evil, stressful places.

The knowledge that his father had somehow contributed to his upbringing made him feel like he could be a good man. He felt that his father perhaps was not as bad as someone in his situation could and would probably be.

Being in prison for almost 18 years had to be tough. His father had spent most of his adult life behind bars. Joel had never met anyone who was in prison, but he knew that it was a place for people who had failed in society and broken its laws.

His mother had never encouraged Joel to do anything in life that he did not want to do, and a few years earlier, he had decided that he wanted to study law. He told his mother that he wanted to make a difference in the world and do something that would allow him to help others.

Since Joel had graduated at the top of his class, he had earned several scholarships to reputable universities, but he had no intention of leaving his mother behind in her current circumstances. He had made the decision to stay by his mother's side until she was well. Even if she didn't ask him to stay, he knew that she needed him.

This was supposed to have been his mother's last surgery, and he was optimistic that she would defeat the cancer. He had learned that there were many women diagnosed with breast cancer who had beaten it. His mother had an excellent chance to survive. She had never smoked in her life and had led a very healthy lifestyle.

He still remembered the day his mother had found the courage to tell him about her condition. He had never seen her break down and cry before. She was a fighter. She had told him that God would look after her, and that if it were her turn to go, she would accept it, and wanted him to do the same. She held so much faith in her heart. She had never cried again after that, and had shown so much courage. Despite her pain and suffering, she always remained optimistic and happy.

His mother had raised him in such a way that he could show God his love, devotion, and faith without having to go inside a church. They had studied the Bible since he was a small child, but the most important thing for her was for him to live life as the Bible taught.

She had always taught him that he could have God in his heart at all times and that he could also talk to God. She told him that he did not need to be inside a church to talk to God and pray to him.

He picked up his father's picture from the bed and stared at it. He wanted so badly to know and understand the man looking at him from the picture. Could he really be the man his mother believed him to be? Could he be trusted? How had prison changed him?

He thought about going to visit him, but he imagined that there would be a process for him to go through so that he could visit him in prison. He wanted to see him. He wanted to meet him and talk to him.

He wondered if his father had any idea of his mother's condition. Did he still love her the way that she loved him? Could that even be possible? His mother had given up most of her youth for a love that would never be. Most of his friends came from broken homes and their mothers had reestablished their lives with new men. His mother had never looked at another man. She had sacrificed the best years of her life, never allowing another man into her life. Nowadays, that was completely unheard of. Society had managed to create a new culture that would benefit everyone. People justified what they did by forgetting about morals or doing the right thing.

He had never really been in love, but he had had crushes on several girls as he was growing up. He had dated a few times, but he had never formed a serious relationship, since his mother had always been the center of his attention.

After he found out that she was sick, he had devoted his extra time to keeping her company and caring for her.

The few girls that he had dated were too immature, and he really didn't want to stay with them. They were all too busy networking, taking selfies, complaining and worrying about their looks. Joel didn't have time to deal with that. It bothered him to hear these beautiful girls complain about their looks when God had blessed them not only with beauty, but also health. They didn't see that. He didn't appreciate their insecurities, and didn't want to be around people who were so into themselves.

He had dated a girl named Monica who really enjoyed reading the same books as he did, so he had thought that they had something in common until they started dating. She had appeared to be smart, witty, and beautiful. He went to pick her up to go watch a movie with some friends, but they were running late because it had taken her so long to get ready. He told her that she looked beautiful, but she just answered that she looked horrible. He didn't say anything after that, but was amazed at her response.

A few minutes after they left, she realized that she had left her cell phone at home. She became hysterical, as if her world were ending. When Joel tried reasoning with her and telling her that they were going to be inside a movie theater and that she would have no need for her cell phone, she would have none of it. She said she would die without her cell phone, so Joel obliged and drove her back home. As soon as she got out of the car and told him to wait for her, he told her not to hurry because he was not going to be waiting for her, and left her standing on the sidewalk. He couldn't begin to understand how a human being would feel that their world would end if they didn't have their cell phone with them. He didn't want to be around someone like that. They never spoke again.

And then there was Amanda. She was beautiful, but she really didn't worry much about her looks. She could wear anything and feel confident; he really liked that. He really enjoyed spending time with her; she was a lot of fun. She wore no makeup and was naturally beautiful.

They both had the same teacher for their American History class and the same assignments, so Joel went over to her house to help her with her homework. They were both sitting in the living room working on their project when her little nine-year-old sister walked in. She was a very friendly nine-year-old, and when Joel started a conversation with her, Amanda began yelling at her sister. The way she was yelling at her sister for no reason went completely against anything that Joel knew and understood. Her tone and her words were cruel.

When Amanda's mom heard her yelling at her sister, she came downstairs and started reproaching Amanda about it. Amanda didn't like it, so she started yelling at her mother, telling her to shut up and not talk to her. Joel could never have imagined that Amanda would be so disrespectful with anyone, let alone her own mother.

Joel could never speak to his mother that way. He loved and respected her, and he would never put her in that situation. If he thought about it, his mother had never yelled at him. She had always taught him that communication was the best thing, and even if they disagreed about something, they would talk about it, not yell at each other. He had walked out of Amanda's house that day and had stopped dating her.

Lastly, there was Amber. She was very popular in school and very conceited, but Joel didn't find this out until after he began dating her. She thought that everyone was beneath her and would only allow a select group of people in her life. She believed that wearing designer clothes was the most important thing in the world, and when Joel found out that her mother had to take out a loan to buy Amber a Louis Vuitton handbag that was more than $2,000, he knew that he wanted no part in her life. She was very self-centered and he felt bad for her, but he didn't want to be around someone like her. He wasn't sure why he had begun dating her, other than her looks and how friendly she was with him at first. He had liked her personality and she was beautiful, but he had no idea that her personality was nothing like he thought.

It was really sad for people to base their self-worth on material things, and somehow most kids grew up believing that this was the standard way of living their life. Joel didn't care about anything that was name brand, and he had learned to be frugal and not waste what little money he earned on material things that would do nothing for him or his future.

His friends would tease him at times about being too mature, saying that he should relax and learn to enjoy life a little more. Joel would tell them that that was exactly what he was trying to do, and he would not allow unnecessary drama into his life. He was not going to waste his time dealing with girls who were insecure, rude, disrespectful, or overly conceited.

He told his friends that it was his choice how he wanted to lead his life. They complained at first that he spent too much time with his mother and not enough with them, and that he didn't know how to relax, but they gave up after a while when they realized that they would not change his mind.

They used to tease him at first, but they all knew his mother well and liked and respected her, and they had felt bad when they found out about her breast cancer. They had always told him that they wished they had the kind of relationship with their own parents that he had with his mother.

His two best friends, Oscar and Eddy, always told him about their challenges at home. Oscar's mother had raised him and his sister as a single mom, but a few years earlier she had married a man who did not care for his stepchildren and often made their life a living hell. His mother did nothing, always siding with her husband.

Despite the situation, Oscar did respect his mother and never disrespected his stepfather, but he had told Joel that he would never allow anything bad to happen to his little sister and that he would always protect her, even if it meant protecting her from her own mother. Joel found that statement very sad, because the parent is the one who is supposed to love and protect the child, and the child should never have to fear the parent.

He often told Joel that he felt that his mother had lost interest in both his sister and him after she had married. Her only focus was her new husband, so Oscar had to take care of himself and his sister. Joel could not understand how a woman could forget her priorities and no longer care about her children, but unfortunately, that was becoming a new trend.

Often, this was one of the main reasons why so many kids were leading lives without guidance, love, support or understanding. They harbored so much hurt because of this rejection, and grew up insecure, resentful, and bitter.

It was sad to see women who had children start a new relationship with a man and completely forget about their children, their needs, and their fears, focusing their time and energy only on the new man. This should never happen. A woman with children should ensure that her children remain a priority in her life if she establishes a new relationship, but that seldom happened.

Many times men did the same thing, or even worse. They would abandon their homes and children and begin new relationships with new women. Even worse, they would father new children and forget about their existing children. The children were the ones to suffer the consequences of the wrong decisions of the adults. But this repeated itself over and over, and more and more children came from broken homes where there was no love or support from one or sometimes both parents.

Often these children would grow to resent their parents and their new siblings who came to take or steal their parents' love and attention. People just don't realize how wrong it is to continue to bring innocent children into this world and forget about their responsibilities as parents. The sad thing is that the story will repeat itself over and again with each new generation, because children will learn from their parents and pick up the same habits. building similar characters.

Eddy, on the other hand, lived with both of his parents. He had a younger brother, and he always told Joel that he knew that his parents didn't love each other. They were always yelling and fighting with each other, and he often wished with all his heart that they would just get a divorce.

Eddy told him several times that he wanted to see his parents happy, even if that meant they would have to live in separate homes. He just did not agree with adults who made a decision to stay together for what they thought was the well-being of the children, when they were actually inflicting more pain on the children by staying together and leading such an unhealthy and unhappy lifestyle.

Eddy confided in Joel that he had often witnessed his parents' misery, and just could not understand why they didn't communicate with each other and openly and honestly discuss how they felt about each other and their marriage. He thought that if his parents learned to communicate with each other, they could potentially save their marriage. He just didn't want to see them live such miserable lives.

He suffered for them, for his brother and for himself. All he wanted was to see his parents genuinely happy, not always pretending to be happy or yelling and screaming at each other.

Joel felt bad for both Oscar and Eddy, and somehow he knew that although his father was not in his life, God had been very good to him by giving him the best mother any child could wish for.

Although he had just turned 18, he had often given advice to both of his friends and kept them out of trouble. He used to think that his upbringing was the same as everyone else's, but actually, his mother had been his best teacher whenever he wanted an answer. Unfortunately, she had to show him how different everyone else was.

His mother had raised him to be humble, noble, and kind, and seeing his mother's strong character, he was quick to take after her. She was a hard worker who managed her finances like no one Joel had ever met. They led a modest life, but he had never lacked for anything he needed. He had told his mother a couple of years earlier that he wanted to work a part-time job. She had been against it at first, saying that she didn't want him to work, preferring for him to stay focused on school. She had given in once he promised to quit his job if it interfered with school.

He had gotten a work permit at the age of 16 and had begun working a part-time job at an ice cream parlor to help his mother cover some of his expenses. He still remembered the very first time he had received a paycheck. His mother took him to the bank and opened a savings account for him. He promised her that for the rest of his life, he would pay himself first before anything or anyone else. Now, thanks to one of his mother's lessons, he had enough money to buy himself a car and pay for it in cash.

He had to admit that his upbringing had been very different from anyone else he knew, and he would always be grateful to his mother for all of the things she had done for him. He was without a doubt the result of everything that she had taught him, and he owed her so much.

He was very anxious to find out how much he was like his father. He put his father's picture to one side, grabbed the shoebox, and put it on his lap. Inside was a row of white envelopes. They were in order, and the postmark on the first envelope was dated 17 years earlier.

His father had written him that first letter so many years ago. So much had happened since then. He wanted to understand who his father really was, and was anxious to read his letters. He felt a sense of calm, all the turmoil that he had endured over the last year faded away, and he felt his heart pure and full of hope. There was so much he needed to understand, and he knew that each of his father's missives would bring him gladness and joy. With a smile, he eagerly turned his attention to the first envelope.

Three

*H*e picked up the first envelope and opened it with trembling hands. Inside were several sheets of paper, and he unfolded each one slowly and carefully. He took a deep breath as he began to read the first page, dated over 17 years earlier:

My dearest Joel,

In less than 24 hours you will be one year old, and I regret with all my heart that I will not be there for you. I miss you and your mother so much, but I have to accept that this is my new life. I have forbidden your mother to ever visit me. I love her too much to expect her to stay by my side when I am facing a life sentence.

I sometimes wake up in the middle of the night and think that I hear you crying, and for an instant I want to run over to your crib and check on you, but then I quickly realize that you are nowhere near, and I pray to our God to always keep you and your mother safe. I can't tell you how much I regret the bad choices that I made in my life, and I have to accept that I am where I am because of myself and my bad decisions. I think about my life and realize my mistakes. In spite of everything, there is one thing that I did do right, and that is you, my perfect child. I pray that one day you will forgive my mistakes and that you will understand me.

Since I will not be there to guide, support, teach, and love you as you deserve, I will write you a missive every year on your birthday and mail it to your mother. Each missive will include a principle about life for you to learn, understand, and master. One day when you are an adult I hope you will receive all my missives. By the time you receive them, you will know them all and lead your life by them. Please know, son, that I love you with all my heart, and that you are and will always be the most important person in my life. You are probably thinking as you are reading this, what would an inmate have to teach or tell you? Why would you want to get advice from an inmate? I will tell you, son, that in the last six months, during which I have not seen you or your mother, I have almost gone insane, but thanks to our God, I was able to survive. I know, you are probably also thinking, "another inmate that found Jesus." I promise you, son, that is not my case. I hope that each of my missives will guide you and help you in your now adult life, and that you continue to live your life the same way that your mother raised you. I also hope that you will teach these missives to anyone who wants to improve their life and learn to live their life to the maximum. Trust me, someone in my circumstances knows how to really value the things in life that truly matter. A sunset, a sunrise, the rain, the beach, family, and of course, freedom, the right to choose, the right to have full control of what you want or don't want to do.

Again, I am so sorry that I will not see your first steps. Please know that you could not have asked for a better mother. Although I will not be in your life, your mother will make sure that you grow up to become a decent, strong, honest, noble, and hardworking man. A man of integrity. I know that if life gave me another chance, this is exactly how I would teach you about life. I would share a different principle with you every year and teach you something new every day, but unfortunately, that is never going to happen. I have sent the same missive to your mom, and she has agreed and promised me that she will allow me to contribute to your upbringing. Each missive will be a life lesson that she will instill in you to master and form as a habit with each passing year.

In this place, there are so many men who made one terrible mistake that cost them their future. You may think that a prison is the last place where you would find any wisdom or good advice, but so many inmates were great men who made dreadful mistakes. Don't get me wrong, son, there is plenty of evil within these walls and inside prisons, but there are also men who are far more honest, noble, hardworking, and decent than a lot of politicians, government officials, police officers, professors, ministers, priests, pastors, and many of those people who are meant to help others in the world but don't. Instead, they are the biggest culprits, because they contribute to most of the chaos in this world. They are greedy, selfish, evil people. Not all of them, but many of them are.

Don't get me wrong, son, I have also met some really great prison guards here who really care about the inmates, who wish they could make a difference in our lives and are committed to helping those who will accept it. They are honest, hardworking, dedicated men, and I have the greatest respect for them.

All I can hope is that I can share some wisdom with you now and that you can learn something from me. I have learned that our greatest mistakes also carry our biggest lessons. I feel like I am so much wiser now, but I have a long way to go. I guess if we all understood that we should think before we act, that would help lead us into mindfulness.

Joel, I have traveled down life's hills and experienced deep sadness, but I have also journeyed high among its peaks and have had the opportunity to experience more happiness than I had a right to. My life was full of blessings and there is so much that I have to be grateful for, but I made more than one mistake.

Making mistakes is how we as humans are supposed to grow. We really are intended to make mistakes, for mistakes bring progress; they teach us about life. We just shouldn't keep repeating the same mistake. I have come to learn, Joel, to turn my wounds into wisdom, and I am allowing my past to serve and teach me.

Most people are most alive when they are living in the unknown, for it's there that anything and everything is possible. It is at this point, son, that you are opening up to the world, and the world will then open up to you.

I have grown wiser in life because of everything I am reading, studying, learning and applying, and I want to share that with you, Joel. I can only hope that each of my missives will awaken the real you, and that each one will inspire you to be the very best version of yourself and who you can become. Know and understand that if you lead a life of integrity, it will be a rich and wonderful life. Never do or say anything that could compromise your integrity. Hang on to it as if your life depended on it, because it will.

I love you, Joel, for as long as my heart is beating.

As Joel finished reading the letter, tears ran down his cheeks. He was a man, but his tears were not a sign of weakness, but of humanity, because his heart felt broken for his father. He had written that letter 17 years earlier, when Joel had turned one year old.

He wanted to meet him and tell him that he had been right about his mother and what an admirable woman she was, and tell him that he wanted to know more about him and who he really was.

Once his mother was well, he would visit his father and tell him in person that he really did not have to read his missives; he knew them by heart. He knew now what his mother had been trying to teach him all those years, but he owed his father that much. If he had taken the time to write the missives, then Joel would take the time to read them. He bent his neck forward and slumped over a little. Wiping his tears with his right hand, he turned the page to the first missive.

Missive 1

"Never lose the inner child within yourself."
*"The secret of genius is to carry the spirit of the child into
old age, which means never losing your enthusiasm."*

– ALDOUS HUXLEY

My beloved Joel,

*Today you turn one year old, and I will not be there to teach and
guide you. I will not witness your first steps or your first words. My dear
son, let me tell you, there is nothing purer or more innocent than a child.
When a human being is first born into this world, there is one thing that
they do not bring with them, and that is fear. As a child, you will never
be afraid to do anything. Your heart and your brain are pure and so innocent, and it is for these reasons that a child must be supervised at all times.*

*It is sad to say that it is our parents, teachers, priests, and society who
teach us about fear. They inflict fear upon us. They will often prevent you
from being or doing something in life because that is what they believe is
right. Someone inflicted that upon them when they were young. If I could
tell you one thing, it is that despite the fact that you will be an adult when
you are reading this missive, I beg you not to lose the inner child within
yourself, and if you think you have lost it, then go find it.*

*From a very young age, we abandon our true selves by ignoring the
way we feel. We are told not to laugh too loud, that we don't laugh enough,
and not to cry. We are even told that is not acceptable to feel sad, and are
often prevented from demonstrating our anger.*

*Our feelings are neither right nor wrong; they are simply our feelings
and a part of our human experience. If you begin to reject your true feelings, you'll begin to shut down parts of yourself, and you will end up losing
your connection with your true self.*

*Fill your mind with passion and excitement, and be happy. Don't lose
your drive and desire and become like most children, whom society has*

contaminated. Instead, be courageous; be strong by being intrepid, adventurous, happy, and brave.

If you sit and observe a small child and their actions, you will see that what I am telling you is true. The child has no limits. The child's mind is meant to be properly cultivated like a lush garden. If instead it is filled with negativity, the child will be led into a mediocre life or even worse.

Most children will run, play, and laugh all day long. They fear nothing and are happy. They do not know or understand life or its meaning.

Children do not harbor resentment in their hearts or minds, and they certainly know nothing about judging people because of the color of their skin, their nationality, their sexuality or so many other things.

If you really analyze a small child, you will soon realize that all small children are upright, sincere, innocent, pure, kind, gentle, faithful, humble, patient, sympathetic, joyous, and full of love. It does not matter what part of the world the child was born in; they are all born like that. Every human being is born with so much potential, and meant to be great and thrive in their lives.

Unfortunately, son, it is often society, your parents, and teachers who will introduce you to all this negativity and contribute to the formation of horrible habits that will eventually result in your character.

As you reach adulthood, don't ever lose that inner child within, because then you will be like everyone else, full of fear and unhappy with life. You will find yourself judging people for any reason, and blaming the entire world for your circumstances.

Do not allow what people say or think of you define who you are destined to become. Live your life full of enthusiasm and find what it is in life that you really want to do, then follow your heart and make it happen.

Just as today on your first birthday you are learning to take your first steps without any fear, only with the desire to learn to walk and master it, that should be your approach in life. Be fearless, son, today and for the rest of your life.

You know that one of the distinguishing differences between a foolish man and a wise man is that the foolish man will neglect the small things in life and will often gloss over them, but the wise man will always pay careful attention to the smallest things in life. Son, this is so important for you to remember.

Never neglect anything, no matter how small it may seem to you. You must always keep things in order and understand that everything matters.

Practice every single day of your life, and just as you took your first steps today, in time you will master walking, and one day you can master anything you set your heart to do. You will always carry with you the spirit of a child who knows no fear and is full of enthusiasm for anything that life may offer.

Any time you feel lost or confused about your current circumstances, take the time to observe small children and let them remind you about being fearless and enthusiastic. Never think about the things you fear; instead, focus your time and energy on your goals, dreams, and aspirations, and always behave as if it were impossible to fail.

Despite my circumstances, son, I also have dreams and goals, and I will never give up on them. I know in my heart that God has forgiven me and has not forgotten me. Since I do not have the privilege of observing small children at their best, I always think about my childhood and growing up with my brothers and sisters. Although we were dirt poor, it was during my childhood that I was happiest.

I have found that the best medicine for our outer turmoil is finding inner peace. Never lose your inner child, Joel, and remember that every process in the material world is also a process of the mind.

Joel finished reading the first missive and realized how many times, as far back as he could remember, his mother had encouraged him to be courageous and never be afraid to try new things.

He had always felt free to express himself and never hold back, and his mother had always reminded him to never give up on a new task or project he was working on. Joel had been about six years old when he began taking martial arts classes, and he was getting a bit discouraged when he realized that he wasn't naturally talented at it. It was his mother who reminded him to never give up on anything he did in life and to do his best in everything he did. She said that if he didn't learn to enjoy even the struggles that he might face, he would have challenges later in life.

From that moment on, Joel never questioned or doubted his own abilities. He learned to really love what he was trying to accomplish, and put his heart and his best effort into everything, but he made sure that he always had fun and enjoyed everything. He never allowed himself to feel like he was going to fail, but focused more on what he was doing or trying to accomplish. Whatever the end result might be, he would still walk away with a smile.

He saw how throughout their childhoods, many of his friends would grow angry and upset when they couldn't accomplish their goals. They got upset because they were focusing only on the end result. When the result was not what they expected, they would grow angry and discouraged. This created insecurity that they carried with them throughout their lives.

When he was 10, Joel had a really good friend named Peter who was on his soccer team, and he considered him one of the best players the team had, if not the best. Unfortunately, Peter's dad was very demanding, and although his son had talent, his father was always pushing him. If he failed to stand out during the game, his father would yell at him and put him down in front of his friends.

He could only image what Peter's future would look like. He would grow up insecure, and unfortunately the person who was supposed to look out for Peter and protect and guide him was the same person who would affect his future in a very negative way.

Joel turned his attention to the next envelope, which contained his father's second missive.

Missive II

"Enrich your imagination daily."
*"Logic will get you from A to B. Imagination
will take you everywhere."*

— ALBERT EINSTEIN

My dearest Joel,

Today you turn two years old, son. The terrible twos, as they say, and again I am so sorry that I don't get a chance to be part of your life. My dearest Joel, how I wish that I could be there to guide you through life. I am sure that not only are you walking, but you must also be running. At the age of two, you are adapting to your surroundings, and people are beginning to influence you as you are forming your own character.

As you read this letter, you are now a man, and perhaps you think that in order to succeed in life you need a skill, education, and experience, but my son, let me tell you that most of the very successful men in history were successful because of their ability to imagine. Imagination is like the workshop where men practice all their plans. At first men may have an impulse, a desire, which once given shape, is finally formed into action through an active imagination.

My son, throughout history there is proof that man can create anything that he can imagine. The only limitation he may have is the lack of development and use of his imagination. Your capacity to imagine may become weak through inaction. You can revive it and sharpen it through use.

Put your imagination to work, son, and begin building a plan or plans for your future. The great leaders of business, industry, finance, and the great artists, musicians, poets and writers achieved greatness because they developed the aptitude of creative imagination. All of the men who have succeeded in life have said that having a definite purpose is the starting point from which a man must begin.

Son, if you are one who believes that hard work and honesty alone will bring you wealth, relinquish that thought. Wealth comes to those who through imagination make definite demands based on the application of definite principles, not by mere chance or luck.

What are you passionate about, son? What are your dreams? Everything begins with the development of an idea. The beginning is so simple. Do not settle for a job that perhaps will make you unhappy over time. Imagine, my son, use your imagination, and once you make up your mind, fill yourself with determination, definiteness of purpose, and the desire to attain your goal, and be very persistent.

Do not allow discouragement, temporary defeat, criticism or perhaps the constant reminder that you are "wasting your time" to get the better of you. Build a burning desire and an obsession to attain your goals. The only person who can keep you from using your imagination is yourself. Remember what Napoleon Hill said, "Whatever the mind of man can conceive and believe, it can achieve."

You are very fortunate to live in the greatest, richest country in the world, a land of so much opportunity for everyone. Most people conform to their daily routine, their jobs, but deep inside they are so unhappy.

The mind is very powerful, and it will do what you want it to do. I really believe that the key to both failure and success is what people think about; this is one of the greatest laws in the universe.

Our emotional state grants us enormous wisdom and carries the awareness of our subconscious minds. And our subconscious minds are our connection to the wisdom of the universe. Our conscious thinking is so restricted, but our subconscious thinking is infinite.

I really believe that men who think nothing will become nothing. You must wonder why, if the mind is so powerful, do I not think my way out of this prison? I have to accept that I made a terrible mistake and I must pay for it. My faith in God does not allow me to lose hope, but to accept what is for now. Deep in my heart I know and feel that one day I will be free, because I think and imagine that day when I will be able to walk out of this place. It may take several years, but I will walk out of here. Even the Bible says that what we sow is what we shall reap, and I have accepted that, son. I have acquired a lot of courage to think positively about all of my problems, and trust me, that is not easy in a place like this.

Every human being wants something and fears something. Use your imagination for the things that you want. Focus on the things that you really desire. Everything begins with a thought.

Look at your surroundings, son, and pick one item. Look at that item, and you will understand that it came to be because it began in someone's mind. Someone thought about it first and decided to build it. That is how imagination works. It begins in your mind.

I am in a place where there is so much evil and stress, and I am surrounded by many bad people and exposed to many bad things. Your time here depends on the state of your mind. I realize and know that physically, I am in prison and trapped, but mentally I feel free. I can go as far as I want. The mind rules over the body.

Freedom is not just a material thing or about enslaving a person using handcuffs or jail. Freedom lies in imagining. Many men feel like they have lost so much, and they act as if they were in prison, yet they are not incarcerated. It is their thoughts that got them there.

Joel, let your imagination guide you to getting to know yourself, your true self, and let your imagination allow you to help you become the best version of yourself, and I promise you, son, that you will find true happiness in your life.

As I sit in this prison cell, I imagine that one day I will be a free man, even though I am serving a life sentence, and I imagine that I will look into your eyes and see the man that I pray you will become. I have to accept that they have taken my physical freedom away from me, son, and I understand that. For now, my mind and my imagination are the only things that no one can ever take away from me. I will continue to use them and fully control them, and as long as I can continue to fully control my imagination and my mind, I will be a free man.

Always use your imagination to get you through life in good times and bad, and let imagination guide you and help you achieve all of your life dreams.

Joel smiled as he finished reading the last sentence of his father's missive. He thought of the many times that his mother had reminded him and challenged him to use his imagination.

It was because of the way that she had raised him and his understanding of the power of the mind that he had learned to manage his mind, and he used his imagination often in his life to help him be successful at a very young age.

Joel analyzed what his father had said about many people leading their lives as if they were imprisoned; as if they could not get out of situations. This was simply because they failed to use the best tool any human being could possess: their mind.

He felt that unfortunately, most people did not think well. Their thoughts were filled only with frustration, worry, anger, discouragement, and so many other negative emotions that originated in the mind.

Joel fully understood what his father had said about being behind bars, yet using his mind to be free. It was amazing how many men throughout history had lived through horrific and unforgettable experiences, like Viktor Frankl, an Austrian neurologist and psychiatrist who was a Holocaust survivor. He wrote a book about his experiences in a concentration camp, and although he had lived in horrific physical conditions, it was through the use and power of his mind that he was able to overcome that part of his life.

When Joel's mother introduced him to the life of Viktor Frankl, he had no doubt that the mind was men's most powerful tool and that he needed to learn to control and master his mind.

Joel sighed and put the paper down. He was so excited that he couldn't wait to see what missive number three would be about. He grabbed the next envelope from the shoebox and tore it open, eager to learn more about his father and who he really was.

Four

Missive III

"Choose your words wisely."
*"Let no unwholesome word proceed from your
mouth, but only such a word as is good for
edification according to the need of the moment,
so that it will give grace to those who hear."*

– EPHESIANS 4:29, *NEW AMERICAN STANDARD BIBLE*

My dearest son,

*I cannot believe that you are now three years old. I can only imagine
how much you have grown, and there is not a day that goes by that I do not
miss you. I imagine that by now you must be talking. At your age, you learn
everything at a very fast pace. I wish I were there to teach you to speak.
Words are magical. It does not matter what language you are speaking;
every word has its own meaning, and each language is unique and beautiful. Most people do not realize that a single word can change the world. A
single word can start a war or end a war. It can save a life or destroy a life.*

*Our words carry massive weight. More weight than we sometimes
realize. Sometimes words can affect people for years, giving them the courage they need to continue or just another reason to give up.*

*Saying the right words at the wrong time can be just as damaging as
saying the wrong words. Many times words are left unsaid, and that can*

be very hurtful. In life, you must learn to know when and if to speak. The right word spoken at the right time will make all the difference for someone.

Every day of our lives, we are shaping reality for someone by the words that we use with them. Words can comfort us when we are feeling sad, inspire us to take action, make us laugh, humiliate us, educate us, and even incite violence.

Words have incited divorces, murders, and fights, and many relationships have failed because of words. In the relationship, someone said too many words, not enough words, and possibly the wrong words. We take our words for granted because we say so many words daily.

Son, make sure you always use the power of your words thoughtfully and positively to help prevent more pain in the world.

With words, we express how we feel mentally, emotionally, and even physically. You have to be very careful with the conversations you have with other people, but also the conversations you have with yourself. The words you use when you are speaking to yourself can be very damaging if they are the wrong ones.

People are creatures of habit, and they will talk to each other about how terrible their lives are, how they hate their jobs, and how miserable they are in their relationships. They often do not realize that because of their words, their circumstances will only become worse. If you want things to change, then you must change your words. Do not talk about the things that frustrate or discourage you. Do not say or speak words about things that you do not want to happen, because the subconscious mind will pick up only the words, not the do, or do not.

There are people who make themselves physically sick just because they are constantly talking about a certain disease. If you are not feeling well, then tell yourself that you are going to get better and you are well. Do not sit there and think about a specific ailment, because when you are thinking about it, you are having a conversation with yourself.

Someone I met years ago once told me that if I did not have anything good to say, then I should not say anything at all. I really believe that the words we say will reveal our thoughts.

Words are magic, son. If you are not happy with your circumstances, then do something about it, but do not talk about the things you do not want to keep happening in your life.

Make sure that the words you use with others will help create smiles, not frowns; laughs, not tears. Never use words to put someone down, but rather to lift them up. Understand the power that words have and use them to inspire, not discourage, to teach the good of the world, not the bad and evil, to say the right words that will demonstrate love, not hate or resentment, and choose the right words that will make a situation better, not worse.

Always be mindful when it comes to the words you use, because often a word you say may not mean a lot to you. but it may to the person hearing it, and it could remain with them for a lifetime, good or bad. Before you say something to someone, think about how you would feel if someone said that to you.

You have to know that on a daily basis, you will encounter people who will do the opposite of everything I am sharing with you. I need you to understand, son, that if someone in your life says something hurtful to you, whatever words they utter can only be hurtful when you allow yourself to believe that those words are truth.

Do not ever allow other people's words to hurt you. Do not give them that power. Understand, son, that most of humanity never thinks at all before they speak because they really do not understand how powerful words are. Now that I have shared this with you, I only hope that you master it, and that the words you share with yourself or the world will help you grow as a human being and make the world a better place.

It was soon after Joel's fifth birthday when his mother explained the power of words to him in detail. She had been talking to him about it before then, but it was not until that day that he really understood what words could do to a person.

Joel and his mother had gone to the YMCA to swim, and they were both in the pool playing as they often did. Joel had met a little boy named Jonathan who was also five years old. Jonathan was very shy and kept to himself, but the moment that Joel met him, he liked him and began talking to him. They immediately became very good friends.

Jonathan's mom was always with him, but she never went in the pool to swim. Joel remembered that she didn't smile at all and always looked angry. Although Joel's mom tried to be friendly with her, she would not give in. Joel couldn't remember Jonathan's mom ever doing anything with him; she just sat on the bench and waited for him.

As Joel was about to get out of the pool to dive back in with his mother, he heard Jonathan's mom yell at him and tell him to hurry and get ready to leave, but what really shocked Joel was that she called Jonathan a "stupid retard." Joel didn't fully understand exactly what Jonathan's mother had said, but he knew it wasn't good.

When they left the YMCA, Joel told his mother what he had heard, trying to understand what Jonathan's mother really meant. His mother not only explained what she had said and how cruel it was, but went into detail with Joel about how Jonathan's mother's words could affect him in the future, because they carried so much power. Jonathan could grow up insecure, believing that he really was what she said. She also told Joel that most likely when Jonathan's mom was young, she had endured the same type of emotional and verbal abuse, or she might even have been experiencing that kind of abuse at that time at home. All she was doing was what most people did, which was to pass it on to her child.

Joel had never forgotten what he learned that day. He fully understood the power that words carried, and was very careful about the things that he said to others and even to himself, because his mother had also explained that to him in detail.

She had told Joel that if he ever had a conversation with himself, which was very likely, it should never be negative. If it ever did become negative, he should learn to change his thoughts, which would get rid of the negative conversation.

As he thought about the last missive and how powerful it really was, Joel realized that his father was a very wise man, and felt very fortunate to have been raised the way he was.

He grabbed the next envelope and started reading the next missive, with an intense desire to keep learning about and better understanding who his father really was.

Missive IV

"Laugh more."

"What soap is to the body; laughter is to the soul."

— YIDDISH PROVERB

My dearest Joel,

You are now four years old. I cannot believe how quickly the time has gone, and I can only imagine that you have grown so much. At your age, you must laugh a lot. Your little mind is learning and growing, but you are at an age where being silly and laughing happens a lot.

My fourth missive to you, son, is about laughter and its importance.

You may think that I would be the last person to tell you that laughter is important, but son, let me tell you that laugher is the best medicine for all of the world's heartaches and headaches. I have not given up on life because I am in a prison cell and have lost my freedom; I always find reasons to laugh. You would be amazed at the men who are locked up in here. They are not all bad; just like me, they made the wrong choices in life and are now paying for it.

There are plenty of inmates who have a great sense of humor, and despite their circumstances, they still hope for a better future. Some of them will be leaving this place soon, and others like me are serving a life sentence, but despite that, they are still as happy as they can be. They always find a reason to laugh, and that includes me, son.

I read a lot. It takes a while for me to have books delivered, but I always have books that entertain me and make me laugh. I read a book about the health benefits of laughter, and one thing that I learned was that when you laugh, you boost your T cells. The T cells are specialized immune system cells just waiting in your body for you to activate them. By laughing, you activate your T cells, which will help you fight off illness.

I also read that when you laugh, it triggers the release of endorphins, which as you may know, are natural painkillers that can make you feel good all over by helping ease chronic pain.

For a child, laughter comes naturally. At your age, everything is funny. Son, as you read this missive, you are now 18 years old. It does not matter how difficult your life is or what challenges you are facing; you must find something that makes you laugh every day.

I would suggest watching your favorite comedy movies back to back to get yourself in a great mood. Do not let life and its routines take laughter from your life. Make sure that you have a great sense of humor and that with the passing of the years you still have that. Never lose your sense of humor.

Now that you are an adult, I can share with you that women will fall in love with a man who can make them laugh. Although it was for a short time, I always made sure that I would say or do something funny that would get your mom laughing. Women are by nature attracted to men who make them smile or laugh.

She told me that one of the many things that she liked about me was that I made her laugh. I can tell you that there is scientific proof that laughter is the best medicine for any human being dealing with a difficult circumstance. I do not know what challenges you will have in the future. I know that today as I write this missive, you are a happy four-year-old, but whatever comes your way, son, don't stop laughing, and share that with everyone, especially your loved ones.

Saying or sharing something funny with a complete stranger is not something that we do, because people would find it strange, but that should not be the case. You should be able to meet someone and share something that will make them laugh.

If you walk up to a stranger, start a conversation with them and say something funny, please know, son, that most people will react to it in a possibly negative way because they do not know you, but do not let that discourage you. Find a million and one reasons to laugh every single day of your life and make others laugh with you.

I learned in one of the many books I have read that if you meet some-one who has no sense of humor, you should avoid them as if they had the plague. You don't want to be around people who lack the joy of a sense of humor. Instead, surround yourself with people who love to laugh and really find joy in living.

Promoting laughter will help improve our moods, make us more creative, and give us a lot more energy. Humor is contagious. Just hearing laughter primes your brain and readies you to smile and join in in the laughter and fun.

One of the best feelings in the world is when you laugh so hard that you feel it in your belly. Laughter helps bring people together and creates amazing connections. When you share laughter, it bonds people and increases happiness and closeness.

More than just a relief from despondency and pain, laughter gives you the courage and strength to find new sources of meaning and hope. Even in the most difficult of times, a laugh or even a simple smile can go a long way toward making you feel better.

I am not telling you to count how many times you laugh each day, but I can tell you that according to one study, the average four-year old will laugh 300 times a day, while the average adult will laugh less than 20 times a day.

Find what will make you laugh, make it part of your day and don't forget to share that with the world, son. I really believe that laughter is a major component of a happy life, and has powerful physical and mental benefits. Everyone is facing something difficult in life, but no matter what it is, you can learn to laugh and really benefit from its healing power.

Find something that makes you happy and brings a smile to your face or makes you laugh, and make sure that you do it on a daily basis. Share your happiness with others, too. It doesn't matter what circumstances or challenges you may face in your future; never allow those challenges to keep you from laughing each day.

Life is too short and goes by too quickly to waste a day without the joy of a great laugh and a warm smile. Learn to master this, son, and it doesn't matter how hard life hits you. If you include laughter in your daily life, it will never keep you down.

Joel couldn't help but smile as he read the missive. Having a great sense of humor and laughing had always been a must in his upbringing. His mother was always in a great mood and would constantly find ways to make him smile.

She had told Joel that even if things weren't going the way he wanted, he must always find a reason to smile. She told him that life could be very challenging at times, and if you allowed the negative things in life to take control of you, they would.

When Joel was 10 years old, he and his mother had gone to pick up some school supplies at the store. As they were leaving, his mother reminded him that she needed to stop by the grocery store to get some things for dinner, but they were pressed for time.

As they were standing in line to pay for the groceries, the man who was standing behind them had one item in his hand, so as his mother often did, she asked him to go ahead of them. What she didn't realize until he put the one item down was that his wife was coming around the corner with a cart completely packed with groceries.

The man could have been honest with his mom and told her that he had a lot more than one item, but instead he took advantage of her generosity. He signaled for his wife to go past Joel and his mom and begin unloading the groceries.

What should have taken only a few minutes took over 15 minutes. When Joel's mom had finally paid and they were leaving the store, instead of being frustrated and upset, she started laughing really hard at what had just happened. When they got to the car, they couldn't stop laughing. What made his mom laugh even more was the look the cashier had given the man after he had paid for his groceries, and how she had said, "How rude was that?" as he was walking away, since she had witnessed everything.

His mom explained to him that most people would have been very angry and frustrated with that situation. Even though she had been in a hurry to get home, her intentions toward the man had been good, and she wasn't about to frustrate herself and ruin her evening by getting mad at him for his actions.

Instead she chose to laugh it off, and told Joel that the man's actions would not keep her from ever letting another person go in front of her at any store. She told Joel that she did the things she did because of how she felt as she did them, and the end result didn't really matter to her.

When they got home and she shut off the car, she turned around and looked at Joel with the same comical expression that the cashier had made as she said, "How rude was that?" Then they both began laughing so hard again that they could feel it in their bellies. Joel knew what his mother had intended to do. She had ensured that it didn't matter how difficult things were going for him; laughter would always follow him because it truly was the best medicine.

Joel got up from his bed and stretched for a moment as he thought about the last missive and all the missives he had read. He realized that he fully understood everything that he was reading and was applying it to his life daily.

He now saw and understood that despite his circumstances, his father was very wise and demonstrated more decency and respect than a lot of people Joel had met in his life.

He thought of his father writing all those missives to him and how passionate he was about each of them, and Joel wanted to make sure that he didn't miss anything. As his mother had asked him to do when he was little, he made every effort to teach and explain his actions to many of his friends, but they just didn't understand.

He walked into the kitchen, grabbed a glass from the cupboard, filled it with water and quickly drank it. He rinsed the glass, dried it and put it back in the cupboard, then headed back to the bedroom to keep reading his father's missives.

Five

Missive V

"Build your own personal library."
*"Reading gives us someplace to go when
we have to stay where we are."*

– MASON COOLEY

My dearest Joel,

You are now five years old. You will start kindergarten this year. I wish with all my heart that I could be there for you on that very special first day of school. I am sure that you will love school.

Kindergarten will give you the opportunity to make new friends and meet the teachers who are going to have a huge influence on your life. Although you will not be reading in kindergarten yet, soon you will get to learn about numbers and letters and eventually you will learn to read and write.

You will get to see that letters are magical when they come together to form words and sentences. You will learn about literature and books in school. I wish with all my heart that I could be there to read to you and help you learn; to read and hear you read your first storybook.

My fifth missive to you is about books and how magical and wonderful they are, and how you need to learn to embrace and love literature at a young age.

You will see that books are magical because they teach you so much. I have to tell you that while reading almost anything will improve your mind, you have to become very selective about the books you read. Books can teach you anything about life that you may want to learn. They often entertain you as they teach you.

My suggestion to you is to read books that will teach you about life and share wisdom, like some of the great philosophers, Epictetus and Confucius. Study and learn poetry by some of the great poets, like William Ernest Henley and Robert Williams, and read the work of some of the great authors, like James Allen, Napoleon Hill, Dale Carnegie, Wallace D. Wattles and Og Mandino. Of course, the greatest book ever written is the Bible. When you read good books, it will be like you are having a conversation with the best men in history.

You can also learn a lot from the great men and women who have changed history and helped humankind, like Mahatma Gandhi, Ben Franklin, Mother Teresa, Nelson Mandela and Abraham Lincoln. So many other great authors that you can find on your own will teach and inspire you to be the very best version of yourself. These authors will share their knowledge and life experiences with you, and you will have the opportunity to enrich your vocabulary as your mind expands with what you read.

The great thinker Judah ben Saul bn Tibbon said, "Make thy books thy companions. Let thy cases and shelves be thy pleasure grounds and gardens."

Reading helps stimulate your brain, since your brain needs to be exercised daily like any other muscle in your body. It reduces stress levels, encourages positive thinking, and even strengthens friendships. Reading can also keep your mind young, and encourage life goals. Books can build your expertise. If you read 100 books in a chosen field, you will most likely end up being an expert in that field.

Reading about someone like Abraham Lincoln who overcame obstacles may motivate you to meet your own personal goals. You will then realize that we are all born to be great and successful and that although life will often bring you challenges, it is overcoming those challenges that will define your true character and who you are meant to be.

Reading books gives you a glimpse of other cultures and places. You will have the opportunity to understand why people are so diverse because of their culture and background, and that will make it so much easier for you to interact or have an intelligent conversation with anyone from any part of the world. The wonderful thing about books is that you can learn anywhere. You can take books anywhere, and reading them can take you places, no matter where you are.

I can tell you that I have loved literature since I was a child, but I never really did much with it because it was not something that was encouraged by my parents. Since I have unfortunately been in prison I have the time to read a lot. One of my favorite quotes to share with you is by A. Edward Norton: "Who was it who said, 'I hold the buying of more books than one can peradventure read, as nothing less than the soul's reaching towards infinity; which is the only thing that raises us above the beasts that perish?' Whoever it was, I agree with him."

The first book that I ever completely read in this place was "The Count of Monte Cristo." After I read that, I realized that I really enjoyed reading books, and now for years I spend most of my time reading. Unlike watching television, reading makes you use your brain, which makes you think more, and you become smarter. Even though I am in this place, I continue to search for wisdom. I have also read the dictionary several times. I have learned so much from reading the dictionary.

People often say they are bored and have nothing to do, but they fail to understand that they can pick up a book and travel anywhere they want to go, because their brain will expand and so will their imagination.

I can tell you from my own experience, son, that books can be life-changing. They were for me. Reading opened my eyes to an entirely new way of thinking that wasn't depressing or gloomy. It really was my first step on my path of choosing my own life and being free of old habitual thought paradigms.

Even in this place, I am learning and growing by reading great books. Books can do so much for you. I continue to read, learn, and grow as a person. It doesn't matter that I spend most of my life in a prison cell. I know and understand that, but I chose to become an educated inmate. I chose to learn and grow despite my circumstances, and it makes me feel better about my surroundings and myself.

Please be very selective about what you read, because it will profoundly affect your life Reading good books will enhance your life and guide you through life.

Make sure that for at least 30 minutes a day you are reading a great book that will help you, teach you about life's challenges and guide you through those challenges.

You can also read books that entertain you, like mysteries, or whatever interests you, but always include books that will help you with your own self development and give you wisdom about life. Don't get caught up reading only fiction for entertainment, but include books that are going to inspire and teach you about life, its challenges and how to overcome them. Of course, read the Bible as much as you can, because it is still the best book written about the history of mankind.

Schedule uninterrupted time every day to sit down and read a book that is going to help you in life. I promise you, son, that if you include this in your daily routine, you will go through life with fewer challenges and gain a lot of wisdom early on. This will prevent heartaches and set the tone for a bright, happy and successful life.

As Joel finished reading the missive, he remembered how he had grown up with books. His mother always made sure that he read every day. When he first learned to read, he didn't want to stop, and his mom encouraged him to read to her. They really enjoyed their time reading together.

The first adult book that Joel read was *The Richest Man in Babylon*, and he had to discuss that book with his mom several times, because he was only nine years old when he read it. His mom told him that she wanted him to have a better understanding of money. Joel had to go back and read it again. He had read that book many times since he was nine, but he read his favorite book when he was 13, which was "*The Alchemist.*"

He had read many different books in his life and his library was extensive. He had a collection of both fiction and non-fiction books, and he would always buy really good old used books. He understood at a very young age that he could learn anything from a book, and always searched for ways to grow and learn as much as he could about everything in life.

His father was right when he recommended that he read every day. It was a way to exercise his mind, and he truly found joy in doing it.

In that moment, as he sat on the bed reading the missives, he realized that his father had made a huge contribution to his upbringing. He knew that if his father hadn't been arrested he might be a different person. But it didn't matter, because things were just as they were and there was nothing Joel or his father could do to change anything.

Joel anxiously opened the next missive that his father had written 12 years earlier.

Missive VI

"Get up early every day."
*"It is well to be up before daybreak, for such habits
contribute to health, wealth, and wisdom."*

– ARISTOTLE

My dearest Joel,

Today you turn six years old. Although I am not there physically for your birthday to share this very special day, you are always in my heart. I can only imagine that you are now a fine young man, and at your age, it is common for you to get up early all of the time.

You are probably getting up very early on weekends to watch your favorite cartoons. I know that I always used to do that. As you get older, you will have the opportunity to understand why it is so important for you to establish the habit of getting up early.

Joel, my sixth missive to you is about getting up early and the benefits of making it a habit in your daily life.

Getting up early is a way for you to reward yourself. The first few hours of the morning seem magical and allow you to experience a deep sense of peace. Being up early gives you the opportunity to have quiet time to yourself during a very important part of your day.

When you rise early, you have the opportunity to think about the previous day, analyze it, and learn from anything that you could have done differently. Perhaps you made decisions that were not the best, and when you have this time to analyze what you did and determine if you should have done things differently, it will teach you how to keep from making those wrong decisions again.

Perhaps you made the right decisions about challenges you faced, and analyzing those decisions will strengthen your character. It will mold you, making you stronger mentally and emotionally.

Son, most people get up every morning with only enough time to get up, get ready, and rush out the door. They would much rather sleep another 30-60 minutes than get up earlier. By rushing every morning, they set the tone for a day that could be disorganized and possibly chaotic.

They are missing so much by rushing every morning. They are not giving themselves the time to enjoy the new day and to be grateful to our Lord for giving us the gift of another day of life.

One of the biggest mistakes people make is constantly rushing. No time to think, appreciate, analyze, and plan. Most of these people walk into work looking disheveled and barely awake, grumpy and behind everyone else.

When you rise early, you give yourself the opportunity not only to meditate about your previous day, but more importantly to meditate about the coming day, to visualize and plan the activities for the day. To set the tone and the mood for how you are going to feel and react to any possible challenges.

Son, rising early takes commitment and willpower, and I promise you that after you do this daily for at least 21 days, it will become a habit.

When you get up early, you should always begin your day with gratitude, and then perform any activity that will help you and make you feel better, mentally, physically, and spiritually.

Ben Franklin said, "Early to bed and early to rise makes a man healthy, wealthy and wise."

With the right mindset, anyone can rise early and be a morning person. Being able to get up early isn't anything new. You have to be consistent about the time that you have decided to get up every day. When your alarm goes off, just spring out of bed and get moving. Don't lie in bed trying to convince yourself to wake up. You must literally spring out of bed. Once you move around and start getting ready, you will wake up and begin to feel better within minutes.

Start an early morning routine. Get up and work out if that is what you decide you will do with your mornings. Whatever you decide to do in the morning, start a routine and stick with it. The morning is a great time to do your daily exercise. It helps you set up your day with energy, motivation and tons of zest. You will feel happier and calmer after you finish exercising.

Most successful people are early risers. Whatever their motivations, they have all reaped the benefits of getting up early to plan their days and set goals.

Most successful people will drag their tired bodies out of bed and start their day very early, while most other people are still sleeping. You must possess the ability to control your inner voice, which will tell you that you are too tired and need to sleep more. If you set your mind to win and do not let yourself listen to that inner voice that is telling you to stay in bed, things will get better. If you can take charge of your inner voice, you will become unstoppable.

By waking up just an hour earlier each morning, you could gain 15 days in a year. You have to think about how many days of your life you want to waste sleeping. You should really reconsider how much wasted time that is, time that could help you work on achieving your goals. We only need six hours of sleep a night. Any more is just wasting life.

Remember, son, that early risers are ahead of everyone because they begin their days feeling calm, collected and accomplished, when most everyone else is rushing to get to work and avoid being late.

Learn to be an early riser so that you can also reap the benefits of experiencing the sunrise, something I hope I will one day experience again. I know that you will master being an early riser and be as successful in life as those successful men and women are.

Joel thought about his sixth birthday and smiled as he remembered that the day before his birthday, his mother had told Joel that he needed to go to bed a little earlier because they were going to get up early the next day for his birthday.

He had been so excited with anticipation that he couldn't fall asleep for a while. When his mother woke him up, she kissed his cheek six times and whispered, "Wake up, birthday boy. Happy Birthday, my dear Joel." As soon as he heard her voice, he sprang out of bed and ran to the bathroom to brush his teeth.

As soon he was dressed and ready, they left the house. When Joel got into the car, he commented on how dark it was and asked his mom what time it was. She responded, "It's the perfect time for you to witness the sunrise, Joel." He was so excited as she drove to the beach that he loved so much. It was on his sixth birthday that his mother introduced him to the magic of experiencing a sunrise.

She had bought Joel his favorite chocolate donut and had made him hot chocolate. He had sat next to his mother drinking hot chocolate and eating his donut as he waited for the sun to rise. That moment would remain in his mind and heart forever.

Joel would never forgot how magical that dawn had been. After the sun had risen, his mother talked to Joel about the importance of getting up early. Since that day, he had always gotten up early, and had been blessed to witness many more sunrises.

He only hoped that one day he would be fortunate enough to share a sunrise with his father. If anyone would really appreciate a sunrise, it would be his father. As he opened the next envelope to read the following missive, he reflected on how wise his father was and how eager he was to keep learning from him.

Six

Missive VII

"Protect yourself."
"Know your enemy and know yourself and you can fight a hundred battles without disaster."

— SUN TZU

My dearest Joel,

You have now celebrated your seventh birthday. I cannot believe how fast time is going. I remember when I was seven years old, and I can tell you that those were the best years of my life.

At this age you are so innocent and trusting that you are vulnerable to others who could potentially hurt you. Joel, my seventh missive to you is about protecting yourself.

In life there are many people who have been hurt and grow up to repeat a pattern of unnecessary pain by hurting others.

At your age it is common to witness or experience bullying by other children in school. First of all, son, you should know that any child who is angry and mean enough to fight with another child is doing it because they themselves are experiencing some form of physical or psychological pain.

Most children are never prepared to deal with bullying and often fall victim to it. Because of their shame and how afraid they feel, most of the time they don't tell anyone, not even their parents, about what is happening. Being bullied can create long-lasting effects that are common in some cases.

Unfortunately, the issue of bullying has plagued many school systems around the world. These children have to deal with the trauma and humiliation of it, sometimes into their adult life.

It's so important to understand why bullying happens, and there has been extensive research conducted by educators and psychologists. Although these two groups use different semantics in explaining why bullying occurs, there is always a common theme: power and control.

It's clear that being raised by abusive or overly strict parents can cause children to mimic what they are learning at home. Another very common cause for children to bully others is that the child lacks attention from a parent at home and learns to lash out at others to get attention.

There are so many children who are neglected by their parents. This can include children of divorced parents or children whose parents are under the influence of drugs or alcohol. Some of these children are often abused physically, mentally, and emotionally.

There also adults who are the wrong type of role models, because they are bullies. These people could be a parent, teacher or even a coach. At times, bullying can stem from a lack of discipline. It is common to see children who are never disciplined act out.

Son, please know that most bullies are insecure, and they will behave and be abusive so that they can feel empowered and secure. You need to know and understand how bullies behave and always stand up for yourself. When a bully knows that they can't intimate or scare you and that you are strong enough to stand up for yourself, they won't bully you anymore.

There is also another type of abuse you must be ready to face if you are ever exposed to it. It is very difficult to talk about sexual abuse, but Joel, I need you to be prepared and fully understand this.

When perpetrators intentionally harm a child physically, psychologically, or sexually, this is a crime known as child abuse.

It's really sad to know that research shows that as many as 93% of children who are abused, are taken advantage of by a family member or someone close to the family. The perpetrator may have a relationship with the child or his or her family, and may be an older sibling, teacher, coach, playmate, family member, instructor, caretaker, priest, or another child's parent.

The abusers can manipulate the child into staying quiet about the sexual abuse by using different strategies. They can often use their position of power over the child to force or intimidate the child. They may also lie to the child and tell them that the activity is normal, or they may make threats if the child refuses to participate or plans to tell his parents or another adult.

Joel, your mom is going to have a conversation with you about this, and she is going to talk to you about your body parts. She will tell you that your private parts should not be touched or looked at by anyone. You will learn that you must never keep any secrets from your mom, and must talk to her about anyone who asks you to keep a secret or who looks at you funny or who hugs or holds you in a way that may make you uncomfortable.

Son, this is not the best missive I have to share with you, but you must learn to keep your guard up and be ready to fight and stand up for yourself against anyone who tries to bully you or abuse you sexually or in any other way. I need you to be prepared to deal with these situations if you are ever exposed to any of them, and make your mind strong enough to never allow it.

When you understand these horrible behaviors, you will be prepared to stand up for yourself as well as for others who may not know what you know and need you. The more you know and understand about these things, the better prepared you will be to deal with them throughout your childhood.

Son, I want to make sure that you are prepared physically and psychologically to deal with any of these issues if you are ever confronted with them. I pray to God that you are never exposed to these terrible things in life, but if you are, you will know what to do, and if you have someone close to you who falls victim to them, please get your mom involved.

I know that educating you on these issues and making you aware of them will prepare you, son, and your childhood will not be disrupted or marred by these horrible acts. Joel, always protect yourself.

As Joel finished reading the missive, he put it down on the bed and remembered how after his seventh birthday dinner, his mother's birthday present had been self-defense classes.

When they got home, she sat down with him in the kitchen and had a very serious conversation with him about bullying and sexual abuse. Joel would be forever grateful that his mother had prepared him mentally, physically, and emotionally to face those issues.

When Joel was in third grade, a boy named Greg who was much taller and heavier than him tried to intimidate and bully him by cursing at him and pushing him. What Greg did not know was that Joel was not going to allow him to do that. Joel already knew and understood bullying, and he knew that deep down Greg was experiencing some sort of personal pain that was making him act out and bully others. Joel stood up to Greg, feeling all the confidence in the world. This in turn prevented Greg from trying to bully anyone else.

Years later, Joel found out that Greg's father was an alcoholic and used to beat him, and that was why Greg was acting out and bullying other children.

Joel knew that if he ever married and had children, he would ensure that they would also be prepared to face any form of bullying or sexual abuse. He felt that all parents should educate their children on these topics. That would prevent so much unnecessary heartache and all the tragedies that were happening, with teenagers even committing suicide because of bullying or because they had fallen victim to sexual abuse.

Joel always spoke to as many people as possible about these topics, and had many times given his friends advice and helped them out of challenging situations.

He got up from the bed and went to check on his mother. He had so much to thank her for. He felt that her parenting had saved him from a lot of pain and heartache.

He stood outside her bedroom door, but didn't hear her at all. He realized that she must have fallen asleep and walked back to his bedroom. He couldn't wait to go on reading his father's missives.

Missive VIII

"Never lose faith."
*"Now faith is the assurance of things hoped
for, the conviction of things not seen."*

– HEBREWS 11:1, *NEW AMERICAN STANDARD BIBLE*

My dearest Joel,

*Today you turn eight years old. I can only imagine how much you are
growing. You must be an inquisitive, energetic young boy. I often wonder
about you, how you feel and what you think about life so far. At your age
you must have developed some interests and hobbies. At this point in your
life, you must know what you like and don't like.*

*You should have the ability to handle social relationships without
much help, and you should have friendships. You should also be able to
take care of yourself, even doing chores at home.*

*I wonder if you know what having faith and living a life filled with
faith means. My eighth missive to you, Joel, is about faith.*

*When you turned three months old, we baptized you in the Catholic
church we used to attend. Even though you were baptized Catholic, I
wonder what religious practice you follow, if any, and how you really feel
about faith and religion. What does faith really mean to you?*

*I grew up thinking that going to church every week and contributing
to the church financially made me a good Christian, but how wrong I
was, because I was leading a life that was completely the opposite of what
Jesus Christ teaches us. At this point in my life, son, even though my circumstances are somewhat difficult, I have not lost my faith in God.*

*I have come to realize that if I were released from prison today, I
would not be part of any institutional religion. I would reject temples and
rituals, and I would instead worship God through my inner statements
and outward qualities. I would lead my life as the Bible teaches us. I*

would do more for others, and through my actions I would show God my love and devotion to him.

Most people spend their entire lives believing that they are demonstrating their faith by being part of a church, congregation, or group, but they are so wrong. They go to church and act the part. As soon as they leave, they go back to their sinful ways. They forget that God is watching all of the time.

They think that as long as they go to church every week and make their weekly financial contributions, they are demonstrating their faith and belief in God, but they tend to forget about God the rest of the week. They forget what he really wants, needs and expects from each of us.

There are good people who go to church every week and also demonstrate their love for God by their behavior. These are great human beings. All religions are meant to be positive and inspire people to love one another, but men are using religion to hurt others instead of helping them. If a religion is teaching mankind to hate or hurt someone else, then mankind should really change religions, because that is not what God wants from us. That's mankind using religion to its own benefit, and has nothing to do with God.

You have the religious fanatics who walk around with a Bible in their hand, and are so obsessed with religion that they often forget to live. They often demonstrate their faith to God by making sacrifices that are completely unnecessary and certainly not what God wants from them. Some of them will even harm others or themselves physically in the name of God.

I can tell you, son, that God loves you and does not want you to harm yourself or anyone else. It doesn't matter what form of religion you practice or follow; God doesn't want harm to come to you or anyone else.

Then you have the nonbelievers. They live their lives in darkness because they don't believe in God. They believe that God does not exist; that we simply evolved, that we became, and that God had nothing to do with that. Those people believe only in evolution.

The most sinister and destructive ideology ever imposed upon the mind of most men is the notion that human beings are but animals, the descendants of other more primitive creatures.

In 1859 Charles Darwin wrote a book, "On the Origin of Species," and since then there have been enormous campaigns to flood the "intellectual market" with evolutionary publicity. Though such ideas by no means originated with Charles Darwin, it was he who popularized evolution more than anyone else.

We now fast forward to our present and find that the theory of evolution has accelerated in power via the media and even the public school system. Today, there is a determined movement for the indoctrination of evolution, and a great percentage of our population have absorbed it into their minds.

So many of these people have pushed evolutionary ideology because they are deterred by the disorderly and sometimes cruel state of the religious world.

Catholics allege that the bread and the wine of "the Eucharist" turn into the body and blood of Jesus Christ, while Protestants disagree. Some say that baptism can be administered only by immersion, while others disagree.

This type of discord on this and so many religious topics has led many to disappointment with religion in general, including a rebellion against divine revelation. This is also written in the Bible. You can find it in John 17:20-21, where our God implied that disunity would produce the opposite effect; i.e. atheism.

Another reason why many so willingly accept evolution as the explanation for mankind is that this allows them to "cut loose" from God and hence be free of moral and religious obligations. These people lead their lives without faith because having faith is commonly associated with religion, and they are nonbelievers or atheists.

First of all, understand the meaning of faith. Most people think that faith is acting as if something is so when it really isn't, and that if we do that long enough, then it will become so. But that is wrong.

Faith is a substance and it's real. It is the evidence of things not seen. Even in our natural world, we have come to realize that there are things that do exist that we can't see.

For example, we can't see the Wi-Fi that gives us access to the internet, but we know that it's there, and it does exist. If you say it isn't real because you can't see it, you are wrong. It is an unseen reality.

If you try to access something on the internet but the Wi-Fi is slow or unresponsive, you become exasperated and upset because you are not getting the response you want. You want immediate access, but sometimes it could be your location or the type of service you are receiving from your internet provider that is keeping you from accessing the internet. In spite of this, you keep the faith that the internet will respond soon.

Likewise, God is real; he does exist. He just can't be seen. He is always there broadcasting all of his power and blessings to you, 24 hours a day, seven days a week. It is never that God can't hear you; it's the way we communicate with God, our lack of faith. Most of us will question why God hasn't answered our prayers yet, and we usually assume that nothing has happened because they haven't been heard.

All that is so wrong. We need to have more faith in God than we have in an internet provider. Pray to God from your heart. There is no right or wrong way to do it, but don't pray to God only when you need him. You should pray and thank God every single day of your life for all of the blessings you have. It doesn't matter what life throws your way; never lose faith.

You don't have to be inside a church to be able to connect with God. You can have a conversation with God whenever and wherever you want. Open yourself up to God and talk to him.

Even under my circumstances I converse with God every day, and have hope that perhaps God will forgive me and give me another chance. Being in a place where there is so much evil, faith in God is what keeps me going. Without faith I would really be lost

There are many men in this place who demonstrate their faith daily and really believe in the power of prayer, but so many more who do not. Son, if you can understand that prison is a place that Satan calls home, because there is so much evil, violence and cruelty, you would have to believe that there is no room for God in this place. But trust me when I tell you that I truly trust and believe in God, and will continue to worship him and pray to him daily because I know that he loves me and has not forgotten me. God is here; God is with me.

I will continue to have faith and believe, because the day I lose my faith, I might as well die. Having faith in nothing means living in darkness. I would much rather be a man who is in prison but living with faith than be a free man who lacks faith.

Son, never lose your faith in God, and make a habit of daily prayer and conversation with God, and I promise you that faith will be the only light you will need to guide you through any moment of darkness you may encounter.

Always believe in the power of prayer, and never, ever under any circumstances should you lose your faith.

You could see faith as the home you want to build. That home must be built on a strong foundation if it is expected to weather all the tests and storms. Faith is the word of God. Please read the scriptures, son, and see how many times you see the word faith.

Never lose your faith in life or in yourself, but more importantly, never lose your faith in God. My faith in God tells me that one day I will meet you and see your mother again. Faith is like oxygen; I need it to survive.

God was everything to his mother, and Joel had developed the same level of faith as she had. God was love and faith, and his mother had always told Joel that God was around him and in him, and that all he needed to do to speak with God was to open his heart. From her, he soon understood the power of faith and prayer. He felt very fortunate to find out that his father felt the same way.

At a very young age, Joel understood that every religion was meant to make moral progress for mankind. He believed in the existence of God and believed that all things were created through "the will of God."

He respected everyone, regardless of their religious beliefs, and never judged anyone. He was introduced to the Bible, and while at first he and his mother attended weekly Mass, after a while they stopped going to church. He never questioned it, since they continued to study the Bible together.

It was when his mother was very ill that Joel felt closer to God than ever, and although he was afraid for his mother's life, he knew that whatever the outcome was, he could not lose his faith. He continued to pray to God for his mother's health.

Joel had learned that having faith and believing in God was a choice, and he chose to believe and love God, demonstrating his love and faith through his actions.

After his mother's first surgery, Father Tim came to visit her several times. He spent some time with her and she really appreciated his visits. He never questioned them about not attending Mass regularly, but instead provided support and prayer.

He had enjoyed speaking with Father Tim, and really appreciated his support. Joel was also comforted by Father Tim's prayers for his mother during his visits and during Mass as he had promised.

He knew that God's love for all mankind was unconditional, since he extends his love to everyone without distinction. Without repentance, faith, and discipleship, people cannot know the redemptive and transforming power of God's love.

His father's last missive clearly demonstrated that he knew God's love and power, and that his faith was bigger than anything Joel had ever known. As he read his father's last paragraph, about faith being as important to him as oxygen, Joel bowed his head and prayed for him.

God was there with him in that moment as he prayed for the man he now knew as his father. As he prayed, he trusted, believed and was confident that one day soon he would meet him. His faith came from within his heart, and before he could see it with his own eyes, he felt that it would soon come. He knew that he could trust in God because he always had the resources to back up his promises.

Having faith in God brought him inner peace. When he said his daily prayers, Joel knew that he would receive many benefits, such as love, joy, peace, and prosperity. Just like his father, faith was as important to him as oxygen.

He reached into the shoebox for the next envelope, and continued to learn more about this man he now knew as his father.

Seven

Missive IX

"Always remain humble."
"Humility is the solid foundation of all virtues."

— Confucius

My dearest Joel,

Today you turn nine years old, and I woke up thinking about you and remembering myself at that age. I remembered myself as a nine-year-old boy and wondered if you are anything like I was. I have to tell you that back then I was a good boy, so innocent and full of dreams. I often wonder how you really are. I have been tempted more than once to call your mother, but I know that it would be unfair to her, because she deserves to be happy, and I imagine at this stage of her life, she may have remarried and you might have siblings.

My ninth missive to you is about humility. A great poet once said that humility is the highest virtue, the mother of them all. Yet society celebrates overconfidence, entitlement, and perpetual focus on the self. It does not promote humility.

I have to tell you, son, that where I find myself, humility is one of the last things you will see, but there are a few locked up in here who are wise and believe in the power of humility. In this place, humility is often seen as a sign of weakness. Only the wise men here know and understand its power.

In your world, people will respond well to humility because it shows that you place yourself at the same level as them, not above them. In prison, everyone acts and believes as if they are better and stronger, than everyone else. It would be wonderful if humility were taught in prison. That would change the culture in the prison system and certainly change the lives of many inmates.

We all know that pride lives and thrives in the heart of every human being, and therefore humility is considered a virtue by both psychologists and theologians. Because humility is often misunderstood and thought of as having a low opinion of one's abilities and self-worth, they suggest that "Humble people are not self-depreciating, but rather accurate in how they regard and present themselves."

I really believe that humility may be motivated by selflessness, but the habit also brings more tangible mental, emotional benefits. I only wish that I had known everything that I now know and understand about being humble when I was younger.

In our culture when I was growing up, you were not considered a real man, but labeled weak and unmanly if you displayed humility. How wrong society in most cultures is and has been, and unfortunately these are not topics that are discussed or taught in a classroom at school. Sadly, we are brought up with wrong habits that we pass down to our children, generation after generation.

The way I know and understand the power of humility, I would say to you that "humility" should be considered your best friend, while "pride" should always be considered your greatest enemy.

Pride and arrogance are obvious among the rich, the powerful, the successful, the famous and even among religious and political leaders, but they are also alive and well in ordinary people like you and I. Sad to say, son, a lot of us do not realize how dangerous they are to our souls and how they hinder our intimacy with God and our relationship with others.

Son, it is so important for you to know about this and gain a clearer understanding of what pride and humility really are, and how to learn to abandon one and embrace the other.

In the Bible, there are many examples of pride and its consequences in people's lives that offer valuable lessons for our own lives.

You can see that at every turn, history has demonstrated how easy it is for pride to increase as we become stronger, more successful, more prosperous, and more recognized in our accomplishments. This is very apparent today in the treacherous pride of some political and business leaders in the world. You can certainly relate pride to the recent worldwide financial crisis. It is quite clear that pride is very dangerous and can produce widespread suffering in society when people who have control and influence are corrupted by it.

Pride can also affect religious people. It is very sad to accept that very few people today seem to be aware of the danger of spiritual pride, but spiritual leaders throughout the history of the church have always seen it as a dreaded disease and a tool of the devil.

Joel, please understand the deep power of being humble with everyone about everything. Jesus Christ said that he was humble and lowly of heart, so he is our perfect example of humility. We must learn to reflect on and adopt the attitude and actions of Jesus, following his example of humility.

The consequences of such an attitude may give us pause. Humbling ourselves could be costly in the workplace, the community, or in other ways. Truly, humility is our greatest and best friend. It increases our hunger for God's word and opens our heart to his spirit.

Humility is not a style that can be acquired in a day, a week, or a month; it is the work of a lifetime, and it is a grace that is precious in the sight of God.

Learn and master humility, Joel; make it your best friend and your greatest companion. Be humble in all that you do and say, and you will feel God's presence and his embrace.

There had been so many people that Joel had met during his life who lacked humility and were arrogant and mean to others. His mother had discussed humility with him many years ago, and that had helped him in many different ways as he was growing up.

As a teenager, he had often witnessed how many kids his age were desperate to fit in and be accepted by others. When other kids rejected or humiliated them, believing and acting as if they were above everyone else, those kids became insecure, which created a huge disruption in their lives.

Joel was always very humble, but he was also very confident. If he ever met anyone who talked down to him, he would just stay away from them. He wanted nothing to do with people who felt superior to others, and didn't want to waste his time and energy talking to them.

Most kids his age were very insecure, and wanted so much to impress the wrong crowd. They longed to be part of something that really didn't have the value that they often gave it.

He couldn't understand how reality shows had become such a huge hit with most people. He thought it was really sad, because most of the people on the shows were arrogant and didn't really have anything to teach. Unfortunately, they were role models to many people in society.

Joel had tried explaining this to many of his friends, but they often didn't understand him, and he felt bad for them. Oscar and Eddy had finally understood what he was saying, and they both knew that if either of them ever treated anyone with disrespect or spoke to them in a superior way, he would not be interested in their friendship.

He couldn't wait to meet his father and ask him all the things he wanted to understand better. He placed the sheet of paper on top of the other missives he had read, and grabbed the next envelope from the shoebox.

Missive X

"Money"

"Some people are so poor; all they have is money."

– UNKNOWN

My dearest Joel,

Today you turn 10 years old, and it seems that with each passing year, you are further away from me than ever. I wish I could say that I will get a chance to see you soon. I know that's not going to happen today, but I have faith that one day I will see you again.

There isn't a day that goes by that I don't wish with all my heart that I could be there for you. As you get older, you will be exposed to so much.

I regret that I am not going to be there to talk to you about the value of money, or rather what society brainwashes people to believe about money. My tenth missive to you is about money.

Does money buy happiness? Many years of research have given us a much deeper understanding of the relationship between what we earn and how we feel. At first glance, it may seem obvious to see that people with higher incomes are happier than those who are struggling to get by.

But as many people dug deeper, recent research suggested that wealth alone does not guarantee or provide a good life. What actually matters more in life than a good income is how people spend their money.

People are led to believe that owning things and having a lot of money is good. They are told that owning properties and expensive cars is good and is what will bring you happiness. This is repeated to all of us again and again until people are convinced and forget what is really important in life.

I have to tell you, son, that I was one of them. I was raised by my father to believe that money and power were the only things in life that mattered. That if you didn't have any money, you wouldn't have any power, and therefore you were a nobody. How wrong was I about that?

73

Most people in life are very confused about the things they want versus the things they need. Big homes and expensive cars you don't need. Food and water you need. People will work themselves to death or make themselves sick working to pay off the debt they incur for the things they want, not need.

In fact, son, it has been proven that when people looked back at their purchases, they realized that experiences actually provided better value. Somehow people tend to believe that experiences are only going to provide temporary happiness, but they actually provide both more happiness and more lasting value.

People will continue buying material things because they are tangible and we believe that we will keep using them. The new house or new outfit will give us a brief thrill, but we soon come to take it for granted.

On the other hand, experiences tend to meet more of our psychological needs. Most of the time, they are shared with other people, giving us a greater sense of connection, and they help us form a big part of our sense of identity.

If I could go back and do it all over again son, I would focus my time and energy on having fewer material things and more on learning to give back to others, sharing and giving. By giving, I don't mean only money, I mean giving time.

I would form youth groups that would focus on giving love and support to all of the young kids who lack good parenting. I would teach them about the things in life that really matter, the things that you will never learn in school because they're not subjects they teach. I would teach them about morals, principles, self-development and self-love.

I would share with them advice about life that would help them build a foundation and a strong character, and help them find success and happiness in life, in exchange for them doing the same for other young men and women who need love, support, guidance and understanding.

Money is necessary to a certain extent, but it should never be the reason for risking your health, your family and your happiness. If you are trying to fit in with wealthy people, they will always look down on you, and if you are trying to impress people who have less than you, they will sometimes resent and envy you.

Rather than focusing on a career that is going to give you a great income, instead find something that you are truly inspired and passionate about and make sure to always give back to your community.

Because money is a necessity to support yourself, when you become an adult and get a job, you need to learn how to manage your money. I want to give you another piece of advice that I hope you will understand and apply. Son, you need to learn to always pay yourself first. What I mean by this is that the day you get a job and receive your first check, I need you to take no less than 10% of your check and pay yourself by saving it.

If you do this from the very first time you are paid and every time thereafter, you will be very well off when you get to be older, and then you will be set for life financially. I am not saying that you will be rich, but then again, I just explained to you that money alone is not what brings you happiness.

I am not telling you to become obsessed with money, but to understand that money will be a necessity, and you will need to learn to manage it at an early age. Never allow anything to prevent you from paying yourself first. Open a savings account and deposit 10% of your check every time you are paid. After you pay yourself you can take care of all of your other financial responsibilities.

Once you have saved a couple thousand dollars, speak to a financial advisor about helping you build your portfolio for your future. They will guide you as to what you need to do to ensure that the money you will work hard for will end up working for you and earning you more money. Remember, you must be consistent with this, son, and never stop paying yourself and depositing money for your future.

Sitting in my cell now, I finally understand the things that matter in life, and I promise you, son, they cost nothing at all. I really believe that the richest people in the world are not the ones who have the most but the ones who need the least.

Don't be brainwashed like most of the world is. Don't try to fit in and impress your friends by buying name-brand clothes or shoes. Material things have the value that you give to them, so don't ever be a follower, son. Instead, be a leader and learn to be better than most by focusing your time and energy on the things in life that truly matter.

There are good people in the world who are very wealthy, but what makes them good is that they are always willing to share and help others, and because of this they continue to thrive and succeed. If it were used wisely, money could do wonders for humanity. Unfortunately, in our world, money is seen as the root of all evil because men make it that, not because it truly is.

Most men are full of greed and envy, and are blind to understanding what really matters in life. Nothing lasts forever, Joel, and I promise you when these men die, they will take nothing with them, and they will leave nothing. No legacy, nothing. Here is one of my favorite quotes about money: "If you want to feel rich, just count all of the gifts you have that money can't buy."

I really wish that I had known and understood all of these things when I was younger. My life would have been so different. But I don't have any regrets. My mistakes have made me the man that I am now, and perhaps one day I will have the opportunity to really appreciate the things in life that truly matter.

Learn to give money the value in your life that it needs to have, but do not allow yourself to fall into the same trap that most people do. You will need to work to generate an income to cover your expenses. Learn to manage your money, and learn to lead a simple life that does not require you to work yourself to death to cover your expenses. Even if you don't have a lot of money, always give and share with those less fortunate than you. Understanding these things will make you a very rich man.

Joel had first been exposed to understanding money when he was nine years old and read the book *The Richest Man in Babylon*. From that book, he had gained some knowledge about money.

On his tenth birthday Joel received a piggy bank from his mother. Although he was too young to think about getting a job or working, he had sometimes mowed the lawn for a few of their neighbors and they had paid him for his service.

The first time Joel got paid, his neighbor paid him $15.00 to mow his lawn. His mom told Joel that he needed to take 10% of his earnings and put them in his piggy bank. He was allowed to use the rest of the money however he wanted, but she wanted him to understand that paying himself first was always a must.

She wanted him to understand the value of money and learn to save at an early age. Joel had continued to mow lawns for many of their neighbors during summer vacations, and he kept saving at least 10% of his earnings. The rest of the money he just gave to his mother, since she would always buy him whatever he needed.

Joel remembered when he had a conversation with Oscar about saving at least 10% of his first paycheck, and Oscar had told him that his mother had taken all of his earnings to help with the household expenses. He had felt so bad for Oscar and had realized how fortunate he was to have such a great mother.

Although he understood why money was necessary, he would never risk his health, his family, or his happiness to pursue money.

Joel's father's greed for money had kept him in his father's business, which had landed him in prison. Although he had finally understood that there were so many other things in life that mattered much more than money, he would continue to paying his debt to society for his wrong choices in life.

Once again, Joel felt very grateful to God and his parents for all of their teachings, and couldn't wait to go on to the next missive.

Eight

Missive XI

"Forgiveness"

*"The weak can never forgive. Forgiveness
is the attribute of the strong."*

– MAHATMA GANDHI

My dearest son,

Joel, today you turn 11 years old. You must be tall and handsome. Perhaps you inherited my height, but what I hope the most is that you inherited your mother's heart. Your mother was probably the kindest person I ever met. She always wanted to see the best in everyone; she believed in her heart that everyone was capable of being good. Unfortunately, my environment tells me differently. She also believed that if a person wanted to change, they could.

My eleventh missive is about forgiveness. I want to talk to you about forgiveness, but of course I will start by asking you for your forgiveness, for letting you and your mother down, for exposing you both to a life without a husband and father. I am so sorry, son.

For the first couple of years that I was in this place, I resented my father so much. I kept thinking back to how our father got us involved in the family business, and I disliked him so much. I blamed him for my misfortune, for my misery, for being locked up in a prison serving a life sentence. I felt such pain and anger in my heart, but I learned the hard way that not forgiving my father was making me more miserable than I already was.

I had to also accept that I was in prison because of my own poor choices. Yes, my father was the one got me into selling drugs, but my love for the money and the power kept me there. I made that choice.

I had to first accept my own mistakes, then forgive myself, and after that, forgive my father. I had to let go of the hurt, the anger, and the resentment. That was really hard for me, knowing that I would never get a chance at a better life.

I would love to tell you that I wish you would never be exposed to hurt, but unfortunately you were exposed to that the moment I left you behind. In life, you will be exposed to hurt through the actions or words of others.

Sometimes this can leave you with a lasting feeling of anger and resentment. This does nothing but harm you.

If you don't learn to forgive, you may be the one who pays most dearly. When you embrace forgiveness, you will have inner peace and hope, and feel grateful and content. I know, son, that is easier said than done, but eventually you will have the wisdom to see why forgiveness should matter more to you than to anyone else. You aren't really forgiving for them; you are learning to forgive for yourself.

Learning to forgive will allow you to have better physical, emotional, and spiritual well-being. Please understand and believe this.

When you learn to forgive, you make a decision to let go of anything that hurt or offended you. I know this will sound odd to you, but at times forgiveness can lead to feelings of understanding, sympathy, empathy, and compassion for the other person. I know that may sound strange coming from someone like me, locked up in this place. I now know and understand that either out there or in here everyone is fighting their own personal war.

Forgiveness doesn't decrease the other person's responsibility for having hurt you; it doesn't lessen or justify the wrong. It brings you an inner peace and helps you grow and go on with your life.

It doesn't matter what life throws your way, son; don't hold grudges, resentment, or anger towards anyone. Holding grudges will only make you angry and bitter, and you may get so wrapped up in those negative feelings that you will not enjoy the present.

In this place there is very little room for forgiveness, but I will tell you, son, that even though I am locked up in here, I will always forgive everyone who has hurt me, because that is what God did for us. I have endured only two incidents since I have been locked up, and although during both of these incidents, other inmates tried to hurt me, I have forgiven them. As a matter of fact, believe it or not, I consider one of them a great friend.

One day I will tell you the story of what happened and why, and you will have a better understanding. Either way, I have never held anger or resentment towards anyone after I reconciled my feelings towards my father, and I can't tell you how great that has been for me, son.

There are so many people in this world who have been abused physically, mentally, and emotionally. Their pain has been so great that they find comfort in hatred and resentment for those who hurt them, and that is truly the worst thing they can do to themselves. Forgiveness is not something we do for other people, but rather something that we do for ourselves to heal and move on.

I also had to learn to forgive myself for the mistakes that I have made in my life, and the people that I have hurt, whether it was intentional or not. For a long time, I was really angry at myself, and I have to tell you, Joel, that I learned the hard way that having self-contempt for all of my mistakes and refusing to let them go and forgive myself was like living in hell. Forgiving yourself is learning to accept and truly love yourself.

One thing is for sure, Joel, and that is that forgiveness may not change the past, but it does broaden the future, and it's one of the greatest gifts you can give yourself.

Forgiveness was something that came easy for Joel, since he had never held a grudge toward anyone. When he turned 16, he had a manager at the ice cream parlor where he worked who constantly kept coaching him about things that really didn't make sense.

At first Joel thought his manager was nice, but as he worked with him, he found out that he wasn't what he appeared to be. One day when Joel and his manager were scheduled to close the ice cream parlor together, his manager had made sure that Joel ran the cash register the entire day.

Joel had thought that was a bit odd, since normally they would be expected to multitask, and his manager had wanted him to handle only the cash transactions. He really didn't think anything of it, but the next day when Joel showed up for work, he was pulled aside by the store manager.

It appeared that Joel's register box was short $300.00 and they wanted to know what had happened to the money. His manager had told the store manager that Joel had been the only one handling the cash register. When he was interviewed, Joel confirmed that he had been the only one who had worked the register, but his manager had also had access to the cash when he turned in that day's business deposit.

They suspended Joel from work for a couple of days as they investigated what had happened to the $300.00. There was no doubt in Joel's mind that his manager had stolen the money and had done all that he could to set him up to take the blame for it.

Joel could have been really angry at his manager for lying about him and setting him up to look like a thief, but all Joel could do was feel bad for him. He discussed it with his mom, and they both agreed that his manager must be having a very challenging life and be very unhappy if he didn't care about damaging a clearly innocent person's reputation by his wrongdoing.

That evening Joel prayed for his manager and asked God to never allow him to become resentful towards anyone. Joel truly felt bad for his manager, because he knew that he was lying.

When they called Joel back to work after two days of suspension, they told him that their investigation had cleared him to come back to work, but they never told him what had happened to the money. His manager didn't show up for work after that, and although they didn't tell him what had really happened, Joel figured out that they had probably terminated him.

That had been Joel's first lesson about holding a grudge or having resent-ment toward someone else, and he never wanted to feel that. He hoped that one day his father would share his story with him.

There was so much he was learning about his father and about himself, he thought as he unfolded the next missive.

Missive XII

"Treasure your body."

"Or do you not know that your body is a temple of the
Holy Spirit who is in you, whom you have from God,
and that you are not your own? For you have been bought
with a price: therefore glorify God in your body."

— 1 CORINTHIANS 6:19, NEW AMERICAN STANDARD BIBLE

My dearest Joel,

Today you turn 12 years old, and I wonder what your first thought and action were today on your birthday. I wonder what your days are like. What you like? What makes you smile and be happy? Are you involved in sports?

Son, there are three things that every single human being must cherish, but often does not, and they are: your body, your mind and your soul.

My twelfth missive to you, Joel, is about what a valuable treasure your body is and the importance of treating your body as it were your greatest treasure, because it is. It's important not only to understand what you are eating, but also your level of activity.

One of the many qualities your mother had was her discipline for exercise. She wasn't always that way. As a matter of fact, she became this way after we met. She would always make sure that no matter how busy her day was, she always made time for exercise. She would actually schedule her exercise for the same time every day so that she would never have an excuse not to exercise. She truly believed that exercising every day was as important as eating, but she was also very selective about what she ate. One day she can tell you her story and how she was struggling with her weight when I first met her.

A while after I met your mother, she had become very slim; even when you were born she went back to her normal weight only a couple of months later. Exercise wasn't important to your mom because it made her look good; she said she exercised every day because she wanted to feel good on the inside. She would joke about it, saying that looking good was just a bonus for working out.

Although I am locked up in this place, I dedicate a couple of hours of my day to exercise. You don't really need a gym to work out. My cell is my gym, and I can tell you, son, that I get a pretty good workout inside this small space. It's my desire to exercise that allows me to see it as possible and make it possible.

I don't really have much choice about the food that I eat in this place, but I truly feel bad for today's society, since I read a lot and I'm convinced that the food industry is purposely creating foods that make people physically addicted, increase their appetite, and make them gain weight and get sick. Unfortunately, it seems that everything is about making money. I have read and learned a lot about this topic, and this is what I have found: Because the food industry consists of publicly traded corporations, they have only one objective, and that is to increase profits. The only way that a food company can increase profits is by producing products at the lowest possible cost and selling as much as they can at a much higher price.

The officers and directors that run these corporations don't care about the health and well-being of the public. The greed that overwhelms them doesn't let them stop. They are only interested in making money and they will do anything to do that, even hurt the public just to make more money.

Some of the ways these corporations increase profits and keep costs down are by using genetic engineering and spraying chemical poisons all over the foods so that crops will not be damaged by disease or insects. They load the soil with chemicals to make plants grow faster, and animals are pumped full of growth hormones to make them grow faster. By making their products cheaper, they are making their products highly toxic.

They also want the public to continue consuming their products, so they have laboratories where chemicals are researched and tested. They are making food addictive. The food increases your appetite, and will actually make you gain weight. This also applies to fast food manufacturers.

There are two common additives which appear to do this: the artificial sweetener aspartame and high fructose corn syrup, which is used as a sweetener. The food industry executives strongly deny these allegations, because they will never admit to any of these facts.

The food industry does not want the public to eat less; they want people to be fat and eat more and more every year, because all they care about is generating more money and increasing their profits. This is also the reason why diet products, in the form of pills, powders, food bars, and prepackaged diet foods will never allow you to lose weight.

They will hire famous people to be their spokespeople for their diet products, and since most people are obsessed with their appearance, they will buy all the diet products advertised in the hope of looking like the spokesperson or model pictured on the diet product.

You don't have to starve yourself, son; you need to educate yourself on what you need to do to eat well and stay healthy. Organic food is the best option, but even if you don't buy organic food, stay away from processed food and fast food, which all contain MSG (monosodium glutamate). This is why people in most other parts of the world eat all sorts of food and don't gain weight. It's not so much the food you consume, son, but all of the ingredients that are used in American food processing.

Son, I can tell you that you can eat a cheeseburger and fries and lose weight, as long as you are using organic products or products with no chemical additives. Please stay away from drinking diet sodas or eating diet food. They truly make you fat. They are loaded with ingredients that will actually make you fatter and physically addicted.

There are no magic pills to make you skinny. All you need to do is ensure that you educate yourself on what you are eating and combine a healthy diet with daily exercise, and you will lead a much healthier life and never become fat and sick.

The world nowadays is very complex, and people need to take the time to study and recognize what they are eating, and how their inactive lives and poor diets will bring on illnesses and diseases later in life that they will not be able to control. People are sicker than ever because of their poor diets and lack of exercise.

Most people today make themselves and their children sick because they are eating the wrong foods and spending too much time sitting in front of the television watching shows that do nothing to improve their life or their health, or playing video games instead of staying active and giving their bodies the exercise they need. Giving their children fast food is the least expensive and quickest way to feed them, but this is so wrong.

The advice I want to give you, son, is to eat the right foods, drink plenty of water and stay away from fast food restaurants and drinking soda. Maintain an active lifestyle so that you can nurture your body with exercise. Do not consume sport drinks, since it has been reported that sport drinks and energy drinks really do not give you energy, but are very unhealthy due to the processing techniques used to manufacture them.

Stay away from smoking, since it is also very addictive and causes cancer and many other diseases. If you are going to consume alcohol as an adult, do it moderately. Every year thousands of people die due to alcohol consumption.

I was reading an article the other day that said that research shows that light or moderate drinking can benefit a person's health, but heavy drinking will increase the risk of high blood pressure, heart disorders, certain cancers and of course, liver disease. Alcohol abuse is just very bad for you and can ruin your life and your health.

Heavy drinkers are also more likely to die in car accidents. I can't tell you how many men I have met here in prison who are serving life sentences because they were driving drunk and were involved in fatal car accidents. This happens daily, son, even as I speak.

Every one of them has a different story, but they all ended up with the same outcome. Every one of them regrets not having listened when they were advised to stay away from drinking. They all have told me that if they could go back and do it all over again, they would never drink, but it is too late for them, son, because they cannot change what has been done.

> *Treat your body as if it really were a temple, and think twice about what you are consuming and how you are rewarding your body with any form of activity to stay active and feel healthy.*
>
> *Cheat whenever you want, if you want ice cream, cookies, cake, chocolate, French fries, pizza, donuts or potato chips. Don't deprive yourself. It's really better to eat something without guilt than to eat it and feel bad about it. Eating foods you want without guilt will keep you thin, but eating foods you want and feeling guilty will make you gain weight. When you decide to cheat, buy those foods from a health food store and buy organic. Just make sure not to include these foods in your everyday diet.*
>
> *You should also reward your body by walking for at least for an hour a day and exercising no less than 30 minutes a day, but if you have the time, make your workout an hour long.*
>
> *I once read a great quote by one of my favorite authors, Jim Rohn. He said, "Take care of your body. It's the only place you have to live." This is so true, but unfortunately most people do not understand it. I hope you will treasure your body so that you can have the chance to lead a long, healthy life.*

As far back as Joel could remember, his mother had always led a very healthy, active lifestyle and so had he. He had no idea that she had ever struggled with her weight. Perhaps one day he would ask her about it.

They would go out all the time for walks and hikes on weekends, and since they were members of the YMCA, his mother would always work out before they swam together.

When he was enrolled in tae kwon do, classes his mother also signed up and was taking the same classes. She really enjoyed the discipline of martial arts, but she would try anything that would teach her to be healthy and active. She also maintained a very healthy diet, and they never consumed processed food or drinks. Their pantry at home was stocked with healthy food, and the refrigerator contained mostly fruits and vegetables.

It was at 12 that Joel began strength training. His mother had encouraged him, saying that it would help him maintain a healthy weight, and later he understood that it increased his confidence and self-esteem.

What Joel really enjoyed was running. He would get up really early and run for miles. The mornings were so full of wonder and magic as he enjoyed the early breeze and the sound of the birds and the wind as he ran.

He could only imagine how his father would feel if he had the opportunity to go for a long run. There were so many things that most people with the freedom to choose and decide often took for granted that Joel truly appreciated and valued.

He hoped that one day he would have the opportunity to enjoy even a simple walk with his father. He couldn't wait to meet him in person, but at that moment, reading his missives and understanding who his father was was enough for him, as he moved on to the next missive.

Nine

Missive XIII

"Drugs"

"Be of sober spirit, be on the alert. Your adversary, the devil, prowls around like a roaring lion, seeking someone to devour."

— 1 Peter 5:8, *New American Standard Bible*

My dearest Joel,

Today you turn 13 years old. You are officially a teenager, and another year has gone by without me being there for you. I have often heard that the teenage years are the most difficult for parents, because you go through so many changes. But I doubt that you are going to give your mother any problems, because if she raised you with strong principles and high morals, then I am sure you are going to be fine.

My thirteenth missive to you, Joel, is about drugs. At your age, I am sure that you have been exposed to drugs. I know that you are probably thinking, how can I discuss this topic with you, since it is because of drugs that I find myself locked up serving a life sentence. I know that I once contributed to the drug chaos that society now faces.

You have no idea how sorry I am that I ever participated in any of that, and how ashamed I have felt to realize what a horrible thing I was doing, but none of that matters anymore, because it will not change what has already been done.

While I do want to warn you about drugs and how bad they are for you, I am sure that I may be a little late in addressing that subject. I really believe that your mother has raised you well and ensured that you knew and understood enough about drugs and how damaging they could be.

I know that most kids your age or even younger than you have tried drugs because of peer pressure and the need to fit in. Others do it because they were curious about how drugs would make them feel, or perhaps they were lonely because their parents were absent from their lives and they felt that drugs could give them comfort.

All of these kids are so wrong about drugs and their use and side effects. Most parents do not educate their children about drugs and what they can really do to them, their brains, and their lives. Sadly, in a lot of cases, the parents are the ones who introduce their own children to drug consumption, since they themselves consume drugs and are often addicts.

Drug consumption is out of control, and everyone seems to be desperate to use drugs to change how they feel about life or themselves. All kinds of people take drugs, the wealthy and the poor, the educated and the uneducated. The only difference is the quality of the drug, but they are all damaging and should not be consumed.

You have doctors, lawyers, judges, police officers, politicians, and all sorts of people, including homeless people, taking drugs. It really is sad to see what we humans are capable of, those who manufacture, distribute and sell the drugs and those who consume the drugs. For this we blame the cartels, like the one I was part of for so many years.

It all comes down to greed and power, son, but I would love tell you that these are the only drugs that you should be concerned about and always stay away from. Unfortunately, there are other drugs that our government has approved that Americans are complacent about and accept as normal. However, many have lost their lives after taking medications that were meant to cure them of an ailment or control a disease.

I have done extensive research on this subject, son, and I have found the following information about drugs and our government. This is what I have found, which has been discussed and published:

It was reported that there should be a criminal indictment against the medical cartel led by the U.S. Food and Drug Administration, the Federal Trade Commission and even our U.S. Congress, for letting over one million men, women, and children die each year. There is clearly corruption within our government that has allowed millions of Americans to die, while taking no action to put a stop to the high medical costs, suffering, and annual deaths, when various proven cures have been made available for many years.

Unfortunately, our so-called "leaders" make decisions for the American public that will affect the lives of millions. They base those decisions on greed for political power and favoring a particular politician, political party or their medical connections, with no regard for the truth or what is truly best for the public.

Millions of Americans continue to die after consuming drugs prescribed by their medical doctors, and this is happening now, son, perpetrated by a corrupt, power-seeking, vicious medical cartel led by the FDA and supported by Congress.

You should know that this medical mess was created by a powerful and corrupt monopoly known as the medical cartel. This consists of large, powerful pharmaceutical companies, hospitals, insurance companies, universities and dozens of other charities, foundations and associations, all politically and "legally" supported by corrupt, self-serving, vicious, lying and uncontrolled medical scoundrels at the FDA.

The FDA has approved painkillers, drugs meant to reduce cholesterol, and medications to control high blood pressure, low blood pressure and irritable bowel syndrome that in many cases have caused kidney failure, heart attacks and even death.

Son, most of the people who need to take these medications have self-inflicted diseases because they abused their bodies by eating too much of the wrong foods, drinking too much alcohol, smoking, and failing to do any type of exercise or physical activity. Now that they are sick, they are at the mercy of doctors who will gladly prescribe medications for them.

People bring most diseases upon themselves because of what they eat, drink, think, and the type of lifestyle they are leading. The body is a beautiful thing, and if you allow it to heal, it will. All you have to do is change your lifestyle and you will not need to depend on any medication.

People are taking medication for depression, but why? If they are so depressed, the solution is simple: change your thoughts, which changes your habits, which then changes your life. Most people who go to therapy because they suffer from depression will walk out of the doctor's office with a prescription for medication. These doctors do nothing to help people; all they do is overmedicate them and make them drug addicts.

Don't get me wrong, son. There have been some huge successes with medicine, since it is sometimes necessary and does help, but any disease caused by what you have been thinking or eating should never be cured with these terrible drugs. These medications will make you dependent on them, make you sicker or kill you, while making the medical cartels very rich. It's a vicious cycle, and very few people really understand what a huge problem it is.

Take care of your body and mind, and you should rarely have to visit a doctor or need to take any medicine. Stay away from medicine unless your life truly depends on it. Eat healthy, exercise, and don't consume anything that could be harmful to your body.

Joel, learn to say no to drugs, all drugs, and continue to educate yourself on all the issues caused by drugs that our world is facing today.

Joel slowly stood up and stepped away from the bed to the window looking out the front of the house. Everything was so quiet and still, and he knew that at that very moment there were many people who were becoming victims by consuming drugs.

What he didn't understand was why people continued to take drugs, whether they were prescribed or not, if they knew and understood that they would harm them. Joel had been aware of everything his father was sharing with him since he was 13.

When Joel turned 13, his mother had a very deep conversation with him about drugs and their effects. She told him that she was not always going to be with him, and that one day soon he would have to make a decision that might negatively affect him. She could only hope that he would never give in to peer pressure and try drugs, but that if he really wanted to experiment with drugs, she would buy them for him, because she never wanted them to have any secrets from each other.

Years later, she had told Joel that when she had offered to buy drugs for him if he wanted to try them, she had prayed to God that he would never take her up on it, because she had no idea what she would have done if he had asked. They had deep trust for each other and Joel never had to hide anything from his mother.

He was glad to know that his father felt ashamed of what he had done and hoped that he continued to think that way. His eyes narrowed as he said softly to himself, "One day I will meet you, Dad, and I know that God will give you another chance to make it up to society and help the world instead of destroying it. I want to be there with you, Dad." He walked back to the bed, sat down, grabbed a bottle of water from his nightstand and took a few gulps. As he replaced the bottle cap, he smiled as he said, "I like who you are, Dad, and I can tell you that I'm proud to be your son. I can't wait to see you in person to share that with you." He reached down and grabbed the envelope that contained the next missive.

Missive XIV

"Don't worry about the things you can't control."
*"There is only one way to happiness and
that is to cease worrying about things which
are beyond the power of our will."*

— EPICTETUS

My dearest Joel,

Another year has gone by and today you turn 14 years old. I wonder if you ever think about me. I also wonder if you ever spoke to your mother about me, and if she kept her promise and told you that I had left your life when you were six months old. Which is true, but it wasn't what I had planned or what I really wanted to do. There are so many things I have wondered about, and I used to just worry endlessly as I sat for hours in my cell thinking about you and your mother.

My fourteenth missive to you, Joel, is about worry. As you may imagine, I have plenty of time to think about all sorts of things, and at first I used to worry about everything in the outside world. It took me a long time to realize that worrying about things that I couldn't control didn't do me or anyone else any good.

People tend to worry because somehow they have lost control of a situation and worrying is their way of coping and gaining control. Spending so much time alone in my cell would drive me crazy if I didn't busy myself doing things that fill my mind with wisdom, and what could be better than reading or writing? So I chose reading over everything else. Remember that books take you places, son. In a place like this you'll either go crazy or grow wise, and I chose the latter.

I read a lot in this place, and one of the things I have read about that I know is true is that it has been proven that most of the things people worry about never come true. Less than 20% of what people think and worry about ever happens.

The biggest problem, my son, is that worrying doesn't actually solve anything, and people waste energy on it that they could better use on things that matter. People worry so much that they lose sleep at night and make themselves tense and often sick because of obsessive worry and lack of sleep.

You could say that I have a lot to worry about in this place, and the most important thing I should worry about is my safety, my life. It's only natural. I'm locked up in here with a lot of angry, evil men who hate themselves and the world, and they will not hesitate at all to harm someone, even if their own lives are at stake.

Honestly, son, I have to tell you that at first I did worry about all of that, but not anymore. You have to learn to distinguish between solvable and unsolvable worries.

You have to ask yourself how often you worry about things that you can't change. This creates unnecessary additional stress on both your body and your mind, and on you. It will actually prevent you from being happy and enjoying your life experiences today. People who learn to let go of worries instead of stressing over them are much healthier than those who do not.

Learning to keep your mind focused on what you're doing now rather than worrying about the things you can't change is very important. I really believe that worrying doesn't prevent or take away whatever troubles you may have tomorrow, but instead steals your happiness today.

It is a complete waste of time to give emotional and mental energy to things that are beyond your control. I know that you are very young, son, but I hope I can get you to understand something. which is that you must never worry about what people think of you. You should never care what people think or say about you, and much less worry about it.

Kids your age will often worry about their appearance, about fitting in, being liked and having friends. This makes you susceptible to equating your self-worth with how well you fit in with your peers. You should never worry about any of these things, son. Learn to keep your mind on positive things and enjoy life. Live a healthy life without worries and I promise you that you will be happy.

Sometimes worrying can be helpful when it spurs you to take action and solve an issue. But if you are anxious about "what ifs" and worst-case scenarios, worry becomes a problem.

It will get tough to be productive in your daily life when you are fretting about things and worry dominates your thoughts. You have to learn to reason with your worries and do everything possible to think and feel positive.

The reality, son, is that emotions are sometimes as complicated as life is, because they do not always make sense and they are not always very pleasant.

Most people rarely live in the present moment. Their minds are always worrying about the past or thinking about the future. None of that is real. What is real is the moment right in front of you. Do not miss that moment, Joel, because that is where your life is, and that is the only thing that matters.

As long as you can understand that you are human, you will learn to accept your feelings. You will be able to experience them without being shocked, and sometimes you can learn to use them to your own benefit. Your attitude about coping with worry and anxiety is very important, so don't fret about things that you can't control, son. Like that old song says, "Don't worry, be happy."

Joel patted the side of the bed as he thought about how at the age of 14 he had learned so much about not worrying, and how he had lost focus when he found out about his mother's cancer. He had not been able to sleep for days after learning about her condition. He had made himself sick with worry.

For days, his mind had taken control of him and all he could think about was everything that could go wrong, and he even thought about losing his mother. Worry had taken control of his life, and now, a year after he had learned of her illness, he realized that his father's missive and his mother's advice about worrying had been right. He should have invested that time in other things that could have improved things for his mother and for him.

He wasn't able to do anything at all for his mom when he was worrying about the situation, and now he knew better than to worry about things that were beyond his control. He wished that he had acquired more maturity and understanding sooner; that way, he would have prevented all of the heartaches he had put himself through.

Life had presented him with a huge lesson, and now he was better prepared than ever to handle worry. No, he wouldn't worry any more.

He wanted to talk to his mother and share all of the missives he had read with her. But first he would have to finish reading them all, he thought as he grabbed the next missive.

Ten

Missive XV

"Be persistent in things that matter."
"Strength does not come from winning. Your struggles develop your strengths. When you go through hardships and decide not to surrender, that is strength."

— MAHATMA GHANDI

My dearest Joel,

You have now celebrated your 15th birthday. I cannot believe how fast time is going. I remember when I was 15 years old, and I can tell you those were some of the best years of my life. I shared such a great relationship with my siblings and I wanted so badly to help my parents out. Unfortunately, at that age, son, I was already selling marijuana for my father.

My little brother came home with chocolate that the school had given him to sell for a fundraiser. He was so excited because he wanted to sell as much chocolate as he could. I asked him what he was going to get in exchange for selling it, and my little brother told me that the grand prize was a bicycle. He really wanted a bike, but he didn't think he had what it would take to win it.

I promised my little brother that I would help him sell all the chocolate and that he would win the bike. Let me tell you son, I had a goal, and I knew that I would keep going until all the chocolate my little brother had was sold. Because of the deep desire I had to make my little brother happy, my persistence paid off, and we sold all the chocolate and my little brother won that bicycle. I can tell you, son, that my desire was bigger than anything else, and when you combine desire with persistence, you can't help but achieve your goals.

At this age, you may be playing sports and learning new things. You will find out that to get better at whatever you are trying to achieve, you must not give up, but be persistent in what you are doing. If you have learned to ride a bike by now, I'm sure that you probably only struggled for a short while to learn, and if you were persistent, you have gotten really good at it.

My fifteenth missive, my son, is about being persistent at anything you want to accomplish and never giving up. All of us have the power and the energy to achieve all of our life goals, and the key agent is desire, but most people don't understand how important it is to have a burning desire to achieve their goals and dreams.

In life, you will come to realize that persistence is a skill that can help you achieve your life goals and get what you want. It can even be a way to assert yourself with difficult or stubborn people.

Showing persistence in any task, goal or interaction will often be what distinguishes those who are successful from those who fail. In fact, a lack of persistence, or quitting and giving up too soon are the most common reasons for failure. Most people give up too soon.

To be persistent, you must always believe in yourself and be very passionate about what you want to achieve in life. Know what makes you passionate. Situations and circumstances in life will always challenge you, so you must learn to choose your battles wisely, which means focusing on what you can really control.

Son, you also have to be really honest with yourself. Before you give up on a goal or a dream, you must be aware of your paradigms and patterns and determine if they are helping or hurting you.

Always be strong enough to learn to break through the walls, and I don't mean physically; I mean mentally and emotionally. Remember that *your thoughts will define what you can overcome. Don't give up! Don't ever allow what anyone thinks or says about you to define who you are.*

No matter what you decide to pursue in life, it is of the utmost importance to do those things persistently. Being persistent is to continue holding an opinion or following a course of action despite difficulty or opposition. The way that you do things, with the outmost care, concentration and true commitment will be your greatest strength. This is a good way for anyone to achieve success in every aspect of life.

You may often become discouraged by others' opinions, or because you don't immediately see the results you want. This could be because you have become afraid of the unknown, but if you have formed the habit of making persistent efforts, this will help you achieve your goals.

Son, don't allow the inner critic that may be inside of you discourage you from pursuing your dreams and goals.

If you possess some talent, that talent alone won't do everything for you. It is important for you remain persistent in addition to using your talent.

Persistence can help you achieve extraordinary success, and if you are persistent, you will not fail in your life or goals. Persistence makes anything possible, and gives you the opportunity to find and reach your success. It means having patience and never giving up.

Most successful people count persistence among their attributes. Although they may have faced difficulties and challenges, they never gave up or quit, and never allowed themselves to lose hope or courage because of adversities or hardships. If they faced failure, they never saw it as a hindrance, but rather as an opportunity to further improve whatever they were doing.

The trait of persistence is highly valued by conscientious overachievers. Things often do not go as planned, and when you are faced with roadblocks, you must remain focused on what lies ahead in order to overcome obstacles and make any necessary adjustments.

Experiencing failures along your path to success does not mean that you have failed. Failure will happen only when you allow those experiences to make you quit.

Persistence creates success. Character is built during repeated attempts. Never give up, son. Martin Luther King, Jr. once said, "If you can't fly then run, if you can't run then walk, if you can't walk then crawl, but whatever you do you have to keep moving forward."

Finally, find out what success means to you on your own terms. Be persistent enough to never give up and you will achieve that success.

I know that you will grow up to be a great man, and that each missive I share with you will hopefully help you achieve all your goals and dreams.

Continue to be persistent in the things that matter. Master your mind by controlling your thoughts and learning to replace negative thoughts with positive ones whenever you are facing a challenge that may prevent you from achieving a specific goal or task. Persistence is refusing to quit; it's looking adversity in the face and telling yourself that you can beat the odds. It's refusing to step aside. Whatever you do, Joel, never give up; always be very persistent in all that you do.

Nothing in the world can take the place of persistence: not talent, genius, or education. Persistence and determination alone are omnipotent.

Set standards for your life that will let you be true to yourself, and take immediate action each day so you can achieve that which you most desire. You must start learning to live your life on your own terms, seizing opportunity, embracing risk and getting to the heart of your desires. You will need patience and endurance to persist and achieve all of your goals and dreams.

Joel knew how important persistence was in achieving goals. The story his father had shared with him about his little brother made him like his dad even more. It appeared that he had always cared deeply about his family and had demonstrated his love for them in many ways.

He had never been one to give up on anything in life. Although he had put college on hold until his mother was declared cancer-free, Joel knew that as soon as he clearly defined his goals, he would have a burning desire to accomplish them. He would be relentless and would not stop until he achieved his dreams.

As he sat on the bed, Joel wondered what his father's greatest goals and dreams had been. He would be sure to ask him whenever he had the chance to meet him and talk to him. One thing he knew for sure, and that was that his greatest desire was for his mother to overcome cancer. He leaned back and rested his head against the headboard as he began reading the next missive.

Missive XVI

"Gratitude"

*"Gratitude is not only the greatest of virtues,
but the parent of all the others."*

— CICERO

My dearest Joel,

Today you turn 16 years old. I wonder if you are now driving and who had the privilege of teaching you to drive. I wonder what kind of driver you are. I continue to miss everything about you, and in my mind I have created a vision of who you are and what you look like.

Although I have missed having you and your mother in my life, since I am still locked up here, I am still so grateful for everything in my life before I came here, and even while I have been here. I think I have many blessings.

I once read a statement by Albert Schweitzer, who said, "To educate yourself for the feeling of gratitude means to take nothing for granted, but to always seek out and value the kindness that stands behind the action. Nothing that is done for you is a matter of course. Everything originates in a will for the good, which is directed at you. Train yourself never to put off the word or action for the expression of gratitude."

This statement is so true, son, and I really believe that a man who leads a life in which there is no gratitude is a man with an empty soul. Despite my circumstances, I am very grateful to God for my life and certainly for a lot of the wonderful things I got to experience before I was arrested. And of course, there is you and your mother. How can I not be grateful?

I really believe that if people would focus on the things in life that really matter and that one should be grateful for, then their lives would very different and quite blessed. People tend to take for granted so many

103

things that they should be grateful for, focusing on the negative. Scientists have also said that gratitude is associated with better health.

People who are thankful for what they have are better able to cope with stress and have a more positive attitude. These are the people who will always achieve their goals.

I really believe that people who show gratitude will get more out of life. My advice to you is to demonstrate gratitude every single day of your life. When you learn to develop an attitude of gratitude, this will help you live a longer and much happier life.

There are many different ways in which people demonstrate gratitude. They can be thankful for past blessings in their life and have great memories of their childhood. They can also be grateful for the present, not taking their good fortune for granted. In addition, they can be grateful and hopeful about their future by maintaining a positive attitude about life.

Son, if you learn to cultivate a sense of gratitude, it will help you refocus your attention on the positive things in your life, rather than the negative and everything that you desire but find lacking in your life.

It may sound strange and even selfish of me to say this to you, but I am grateful that I was arrested and put behind bars, even though it meant not being able to be with you and your mother, who I love so much. If I had to be honest with myself, and I have been, I know that if I hadn't been arrested, I would probably be dead by now.

The lifestyle I was leading was very bad, and while I never killed anyone, I came very close to losing my life a few times. Getting arrested made me walk away from a lifestyle that would have eventually destroyed me. Although I feel that my sentence was too severe and did not fit the crime, I am grateful that I was caught.

I am still grateful to God for so many things in life that I still have, and despite my circumstances. I feel very fortunate to have them. Gratitude is so important because it reminds you of the things that you do have, rather than focusing on the things you want that you may not have.

Practice gratitude daily by starting off your day thinking of all of the things you have to be grateful for; that will put your mind on the right track. Remember to always say "thank you" to everyone, to God and to the entire universe. Doing this every morning will help you set a positive tone for your day.

Before Joel knew who his father was, he was full of gratitude. Shortly after his 17th birthday, when his mother told him that she had been diagnosed with cancer, she made him take stock of all of the wonderful things he had in life and promise her that he would always thank God for all of those things, every day.

She wanted to make sure that Joel stayed focused on the important things in his life that he needed to appreciate and be grateful for. She told Joel that she didn't know what would happen with her medical condition, but that she needed to know that if things didn't go the way they both hoped they would, that he would accept the outcome and be grateful to God for the many great years they had shared together.

She made him understand that he needed to always be grateful for the things that he had, and the experiences and moments they had lived and shared together. That was better than focusing only on what he wanted, because that could lead to feeling discouraged and forgetting to demonstrate gratitude.

Gratitude was very important to Joel and he practiced it daily. He silently thanked God for another year of life, for his mother's life and for his father. It didn't matter what happened in his life; Joel would always be grateful for everything. He turned to open the next missive and begin reading.

Eleven

Missive XVII

"Take responsibility for your actions."
"Man is buffeted by circumstances so long as he believes himself to be the creature of outside conditions…"

— JAMES ALLEN

My dearest Joel,

As I sit here writing this letter, I think about how quickly the years have gone by. How I wish with all my heart that things would be different for all of us, but I accepted my reality a long time ago.

I take full responsibility for everything, good and bad, that has happened in my life. Many of the inmates that I speak with always blame everyone else for their circumstances. They are clearly in denial, for it was their choices and actions in life that got them where they are. There are but a few men that I have met throughout the years who have taken full responsibility for their circumstances. I admire these men, son.

Society has always held an attitude of victimization, and one way or another people continue to claim that they are victims of some outside force. Unfortunately, nowadays things are getting worse, as people try to justify everything that has gone wrong in their lives by playing the victim.

You have to remember, Joel, that every action has a reaction. If you have a situation in which you feel like you have failed, you cannot give

power to your circumstances, because I can assure you, son, that your cir-
cumstances will then get worse.

You have to learn early in life that you are responsible for everything,
good or bad, that may happen to you. In order to get full control over your
circumstances, you must take personal responsibility for where you are.

Self-control is about personal responsibility, self-discovery, and creat-
ing value in the world by being the people that we become. Too many
people will spend their entire lives blaming others for all that is going
wrong in their lives.

Blaming others for our unfortunate circumstances is nothing more
than excusing ourselves. It's a very sad way to live your life, because all you
are doing is playing the victim.

There is an inmate I met a few years ago who blamed his parents,
his wife, his boss, and even the weather for what had happened to him.
You see, son, this inmate had very wealthy parents and was brought up
in an environment where he was provided any and all material things he
needed or desired in life.

He grew up with the idea that as long as you had money in life,
nothing else mattered. If you had no money, you were nobody. Shortly
after he graduated from Harvard, he got a job with a very successful
financial firm as a stockbroker, mostly because of his parents' influence.
He loved money and worked managing money. To this man, money was
his only God.

When he grew older, after making partner with his financial firm,
he married a woman whom he claims he loved very much, and she loved
him. He provided her with a very lavish lifestyle, and money was never a
concern for her. He, like his parents, gave her all of the material things in
life she asked for. They lived in a mansion, drove exotic cars, traveled a lot,
and even owned their own yacht.

When the recession hit after he had been married for a few years, he
lost his job and most of his investments created huge losses for him. It was
really hard for him to find another job, even with his parents' influence.
Because of the lifestyle that he was accustomed to, it wasn't long before he

ran out of money, because he had no income and had continued spending money as if he were working.

His wife, who he believed loved him so much, threatened to divorce him if he couldn't provide the lifestyle that she had grown accustomed to. As the weeks and months passed, he grew very frustrated, angry and bitter. To keep his wife from leaving him, he decided to kill her, and collected her life insurance.

At first he thought he was going to get away with murder, but he was arrested, tried and found guilty. He refused to take responsibility for what he had done. He felt that everyone was to blame but him. Let me tell you another thing about justice, son: This man will only serve an eight-year sentence for what he did, and he took a human life.

It seems that most people go through life feeling as if they have been victims of some kind of circumstance and feel some sort of entitlement. When things don't work out for them, they don't take responsibility.

Stop blaming your parents because they didn't give you a great child-hood, or because they were alcoholics, drug addicts, or abusive. At some point you must break that barrier and understand that you have to make your own choices in life, and that if you make a mistake, you must take responsibility for it. When you learn to accept your mistakes, you are grow-ing as a human being.

You need to learn to own your good and bad choices in life, son, and never blame anyone for anything. Instead, look at yourself in the mirror and accept responsibility, learn from your mistakes and move on.

I truly believe that every person finds themselves in the circumstances they are facing because of their own decisions and their own actions, good or bad.

Son, hopefully you will lead a righteous life in which you will have very little to hold yourself responsible for, but if you do make a mistake, then accept responsibility, learn from it and move on with your life.

So many times throughout high school, many of Joel's friends had blamed their parents for the way they felt about life. While he did understand that perhaps their parents had not given them a good foundation, he also felt that his friends were old enough to change the way they felt about life and even about themselves.

It just seemed that it was easier to play the victim and justify bad behavior than to accept that everyone should be held accountable for his or her own life choices and circumstances.

Joel was very appreciative for everything his mother had taught him, what he had learned from her, and for who he was as well as who he was not. He felt that taking responsibility for the things that went wrong in life would make people realize their true wrongdoings and allow them to improve their lives.

He was glad to hear that his father accepted responsibility for his current circumstances and that he blamed no one but himself for everything that had gone wrong in his life.

Joel laid the paper down on top of the other missives he had read and grabbed the last missive his father had sent him.

Missive XVIII

"Life's regrets"

"Brethren, I do not regard myself as having laid hold of it yet; but one thing I do: forgetting what lies behind and reaching forward to what lies ahead, I press on toward the goal for the prize of the upward call of God in Christ Jesus. Let us, therefore, as many as are perfect, have this attitude; and if in anything you have a different attitude, God will reveal that also to you; however, let us keep living by that same standard to which we have attained."

– PHILIPPIANS 3:13-16, *NEW AMERICAN STANDARD BIBLE*

My dearest son,

Joel, you are now 18 years old. How quickly the years have gone by, and how much I have missed out on because of my actions. As I sit here in my cell writing the last of my missives to you, you would think I would have many regrets, but in spite of everything, I have learned to live life without regrets. Let me tell you, that is very hard to do, but if you want to have a fulfilling life, you must learn to do this.

My eighteenth and most important missive to you, Joel, is about life's regrets. As humans, we will make wrong choices and mistakes many times in our lives, but it is by making these mistakes that we learn and grow. No one likes failing, making a mistake, making the wrong decision about something, saying the wrong thing or being rejected. However, all of these are natural and necessary parts of the process called life.

Son, if you want to live a life free of regrets, then simply decide what you really want out of life and go out and get it. Think about what you want your life to be like, work towards achieving your life's goals, and never give up.

We all have something in our minds from the past that we wish we could have done differently, or perhaps something we wish we hadn't done.

Filling your mind with regrets about your mistakes is not going to change anything. What is done is done.

First of all, son, you must have a full understanding of the meaning of regret, which is: a feeling of sadness, repentance, or disappointment over something that has happened or been done. Life is too short to live your life with regrets. The good thing is that the only person who can force you to live a life of regrets is yourself.

To avoid living your life with regrets, you must understand how important it is for you to give your life some sort of purpose. When you are living your life with purpose, you have the courage to make your own path and truly love what you do to better yourself. Every day you invest a little bit of time in self-improvement, in learning and growing. Listen to your heart and follow your dreams so that you will never have to regret not doing something you really wanted to do.

Joel, take advantage of each day, because every day is a new beginning. Your future is not determined by where you have been, the mistakes you have made, or how many times you have failed. It's about where you are about to go, and that is based on what you decide to do with your life every day.

No matter how hard life may seem and no matter what happens to you, don't give up on your dreams and your ability to reach them. Don't live your life based on what you should have done or been. Always keep looking forward. Never waste time looking backwards, because that's not where you are going.

Being locked up in this place, you would think that I live my life with regrets, but I really don't any more, son. I did for a very long time, but after a while I realized that feeling that way was getting me nowhere. For years, I tortured myself, always regretting my actions, my wrong decisions, the things I had wanted to do but didn't, and the things I did but shouldn't have, and everything that had led me to this place.

I still have hope that something may change for me, that perhaps in the future a new law may be passed that would give me a chance to get out of here, but for now I am just living my life as best I can.

I have met men in this place who have been here for over 30 years, and the wisdom they have acquired is very impressive. One of the things they share with me is that they have accepted their lives as they are, and have nothing they regret at this point in their lives. But there are so many people out there who are missing out on living their real lives because they are stuck living in the past and regretting everything they have done or failed to do.

Son, let me tell you that I am more of a free man than the ones out there who have created prisons in their own minds because they are stuck and incapable of going on with their lives because of their regrets.

There are three biblical components of learning to live your life without regrets. The first is learning to resolve your past, the second is living proactively in the present, and the third is leaning with vision into the future.

Learn to live a live without regrets and you will have a chance to enjoy your present and an even better chance to live a bright future.

I often sit in my cell and think about what could have been, and I have to stop myself from having those thoughts because they are not going to lead me anywhere. What is done is done, and I cannot undo it. I would much rather use that time for prayer so that I can continue in my faith that God is going to forgive me for my actions and that one day I am going to walk out of this place.

Master living a life without regrets, son, and your life will be truly fulfilled and blessed. It took me a long time to realize that if you see the mistakes you have made as lessons instead, you will take those negative experiences and turn them into opportunities, and then you will learn and grow.

When we are faced with life's challenges, we need to use our strengths. Never regret anything, son; learn from it and move on. Even the worst experience in life will offer a lesson, and I have found that a lot of people have grown the most from trying experiences.

Always keep in mind, Joel, that when one door closes, another door will open. Never allow yourself to live a life of regrets.

Son, this is my last missive to you, and it makes me a bit sad, because I always looked forward to preparing a missive for you each year, and I always learned and grew more as a human being as I wrote each missive.

I know that although I am facing a life sentence, I will leave this place soon. Something will change for me, and God will give me the opportunity that I have prayed for.

I have enclosed an application for you to complete. It's a visitor's application, in case you would like to meet me. It would be an honor for me to see you, my son, if you can forgive me for letting you and your mother down and will allow me to be part of your life. At this stage in your life, you have built the foundation of the man you are destined to become, and who I am and my circumstances should not cast a shadow on you.

Please know, son, that I love you more than any words in the dictionary could describe. In the same way, I love your mother and will always love her for the woman she was the moment she came into my life and the woman that she has become.

If you choose not to visit me, I will understand that. I truly expect nothing, but I would be lying to you if I did not tell you that I do hope that you will not be ashamed of me and will not resent and reject me.

You can also write to me if you choose not to see or visit me. If you would like to, please write me back.

Joel, if you can read each missive that I sent you again and again and ensure that they are part of your life and are now habits, you are destined for greatness. Live your life to the fullest.

Twelve

Joel put the last piece of paper that he was holding on his bed and took a deep breath. All of the missives lay in a stack, one on top of the other. He tipped his head back and stared at the ceiling for a moment, thrusting his chest out, his eyes wide and glowing, with a grin that he could not contain.

Now everything made sense to him. He had so many memories of his childhood, especially how his mother spoke to him on his birthday every year. He had always felt like he was learning so much with each passing year. He had thought that everyone was like that, but with time he found out that his mom was unique.

She always seemed to test him to see if he understood what she was teaching him and if he saw the value in what she was sharing with him. She wanted to make sure that he really understood and applied each principle she was teaching him.

He now understood why he woke up with so much energy and enthusiasm every day, and was always full of gratitude, even with his mother's medical condition. It was how he had been raised. He now felt mixed emotions about everything that was happening, but one thing he was sure of, and that was that he was not angry at his father and didn't hold any resentment towards him.

His father had made a serious mistake and had been paying for it for many years. He owed society nothing, since he had spent most of his adult life behind bars and was still in prison.

His friends had always labeled him as "different" and sometimes "weird" because of the way he saw things and handled issues, but deep down they appreciated and valued his friendship. Joel always felt much more mature than all his friends. He never knew why he was that way, but he now understood much more.

Oscar and Eddy were his childhood friends, and they both trusted Joel on any advice he could give them. They knew that Joel cared about them and would do anything to help them.

They both had shared with him that they did not know what they would have done without his friendship, and always sought his advice. If they wanted to drink or smoke, they knew better than to ask Joel to join them, because they already knew he would say no, and they respected who he was. There never was any peer pressure, and that was what made their friendship so great. They respected each other and who they were.

Joel had told them how he felt about liquor and cigarettes, and had encouraged them both not to smoke or drink, but they occasionally still did, so Joel also respected who they were and what they did. It did not make them bad; he just wished they would have more love and respect for their bodies. He had learned to let them be, as long as they did not abuse these substances.

Joel was experiencing a beautiful emotion about his father building up in his chest. He no doubt was an extraordinary man who had made one serious mistake that had cost him his future. He was amazed at all of the wisdom his father had to share with him and only wished that he could have been part of his life. Nevertheless, he did not regret anything, because living his life without regrets was something he had learned early on.

Since he was a small child, his mother had told him that once he understood and accepted that life was very short and that time was very limited, he would appreciate life and make the best of every moment and every new day. Joel knew that lesson had also come from his father.

He glanced at all of the letters that his father had mailed him over the years, and felt so much gratitude towards both of his parents. He had always thought this mother was an amazing woman, but learning the truth about his father made him love, admire, and respect her even more.

He imagined what his father looked like and pictured him sitting in his cell reading and writing all those letters. He had to be so courageous to maintain such a vibrant spirit and understand life and appreciate it as it was. He kept living it to the fullest even though he had lost what a man should never lose, his freedom.

No living creature was meant to live behind bars, not even animals. That was an unnatural thing. All living creatures, especially humans, were meant to live and run freely, to enjoy life, to be able to go out and look up at the sky and appreciate the beauty of the stars and the magic of the sun rising and setting. That should never be taken from any living creature, but everyone who was behind bars had lost it the moment their freedom fell into the hands of others and was taken from them.

When he was seven years old, Joel had gone on a field trip with his classmates. They took them to the zoo. He could still remember how he felt when he first entered the zoo. He and his classmates were so excited, and as soon as they got off the bus, they were very happy and could not wait to go into the zoo and have fun.

While Joel did enjoy being out with his friends on a field trip, he did not like or enjoy the zoo at all. When he got home, his mom was waiting for him to hear all about his trip, and he told her what he really felt.

"Did you have fun, Joel?"

"It was nice, Mom, but I really didn't like the zoo."

"Why didn't you like it, Joel?"

"Mom, all of the animals in the zoo looked so sad. Why would we take them from their homes and put them behind bars inside cages?"

"That's a great question, Joel. I ask myself the same thing."

"Do you like the zoo, Mom?" he asked eagerly.

"I really don't, son."

"Why don't you like it?"

"For the same exact reasons that you didn't like it. Animals don't belong in cages; no living creature does. God didn't intend for any of us to live like that. I'm so proud of you, Joel. I don't want to impose anything on you, and I would much rather you have the opportunity to explore some things in life and make your own choices about certain things; how you see them and how you feel about them," she said with a big smile.

"What do you mean, Mom?"

"Well son, I never liked the zoo very much, but I didn't want you not to like it just because I didn't. I want you to make certain choices about life that will define your character; define you. Does that make sense to you, Joel?"

"Yes it does, Mom."

"You are a very special boy, Joel." She smiled tenderly as she spoke.

"I thought I was weird, Mom."

"You're not weird, Joel. I'm just amazed at that fact that as a seven-year-old you can see and understand the cruelty of having animals locked in cages. Personally, I will never visit a zoo. If it were up to me, I would close all the zoos in the world and set all the animals free, put them back where they belong, but unfortunately, son, they're just a business to the people that own them, and all they care about is making money."

"That's sad, Mom. The little animals haven't done anything wrong; they should be free. How would those men feel if they were put in a cage, even if they had done nothing wrong?"

"I know what you mean, son, but men's greed is by far greater than anything that is good and natural for all living creatures, especially for animals."

Joel had never forgotten that conversation with his mom. She really cared about humanity and loved all living creatures, and wanted to make a difference. She was truly extraordinary, and he was so blessed to be able to call her his mother.

He had come to know her as a very strong, kindhearted, loving person, and despite her medical condition, she always showed faith and gratitude to God, and did not fear death. She had told him recently that until you learn to die, you will never really learn to live. She had discussed death with him like never before. Joel was beginning to understand it better than ever.

He had been sitting next to her on her bed. She had asked Joel to come into her room because she needed to speak with him.

"Joel, do you know what one of the greatest mysteries is for mankind, that they have never found an answer for?"

"I'm not sure, Mom."

"Death, son. Mankind has always tried to figure out what really happens after death, and because they really don't know, they fear death."

"Do you fear death, Mom?"

"Good heavens Joel; no, I don't." She beamed at him. "Under my circumstances, I guess people would expect that I should show some sort of fear, but I really don't, son. My faith in God is all I need, but I really believe that when you think about death and you embrace it, not fear it, you learn to appreciate life more and you live a better life."

"How do you embrace death, Mom?"

"It's simple, son. First of all, all of us are born with a life sentence. We all know that we're going to die, but most people don't know when they're going to die and somehow think that they will live forever. For me, it's simple. I know that I'm sick and I may soon die because of that, or for any other reason that has nothing to do with my disease. Either way, son, I embrace death. I appreciate every little detail about life and am very grateful to God, but more importantly, I make sure that I'm at peace with God, myself, my loved ones and the world. Life is truly composed of moments, and if we let those moments pass us by, we're not living life at all. You must learn to appreciate every moment."

"That's crazy, Mom."

"Why do you say that, Joel?"

"I had never really thought about that."

"You should learn to accept and embrace death, Joel, and trust me, that will make you appreciate life more. I'm not telling you to become obsessed with death, but I am telling you that you should learn to live your life as if today were your last day, because it may very well be, and you will learn to truly focus on all of the things in life that matter."

"I guess it does make sense, Mom. I remember Mrs. Smith, my math teacher when I was a sophomore. Her younger sister died in a tragic car accident, and Mrs. Smith was brokenhearted over her death, but what she shared with us in class was the regret that she was probably going to carry with her all her life. That was that she had had an argument with her sister months before, and they had never spoken again. She was so sad that she didn't get a chance to tell her sister how much she loved her and how sorry she was about the argument."

"How did you feel about her story, Joel?"

"It made me sad for her, but I really didn't think much about it, since I don't ever have arguments or hold resentments towards anyone."

"Do you think that if either sister would have embraced the possibility of death, they would have stayed angry at each other?"

"No I don't think so, Mom. I believe they would have made up immediately."

"Please always remember that, Joel. Live your life to the fullest, but always be at peace with God, yourself, and everyone around you, and you'll be fine. You need to make sure that you always keep in mind that a day without love and laughter is a day without life. Never forget the importance of living with unrestrained excitement despite your circumstances."

Joel had left her bedroom that day feeling better about life in general, but more importantly, he had heard what his mother had shared with him and was learning to understand the great mystery of death and how to really embrace it.

She would always tell Joel that she did not want to know that he worried about her, and reminded him about how worrying only made things worse. She would always say, "Worrying is negative energy, son, and we do not allow negative energy into our lives." And then she would smile at him.

There had been so many times when Joel had expected his mother to cry or break down, but it was during those times that she would always find something to make them laugh. She would play their favorite comedy movie and they would laugh until they couldn't laugh any more.

She would tell him that as long as they were both alive, they would always be happy and enjoy life, despite what she was going through. She did not allow Joel to be depressed about her being sick. Instead she focused her energy on making him smile, and that made her happy and helped her feel better.

He had always admired his mother's humility, and truly respected her because of the way she treated people, even strangers. She possessed something really genuine and special that made her shine.

Joel chuckled to himself when he thought about how healthy his mother had been and how she had always maintained a healthy diet. They loved pizza and hamburgers, but they would only treat themselves to eating them once in a while, and of course there were the freshly baked donuts.

Twice a month they would go buy donuts, and truly enjoy them. His mother would say to him, "Joel, I feel like today is going to be our cheat day." And she would smile at him and ask him what sort of cheat food he was craving that day. She would tell him that a "cheat day" was necessary in everyone's diet, and that it was meant to compensate yourself for maintaining a healthy, well-balanced diet and exercising regularly.

Joel had played sports his entire life, and made the varsity soccer team when he was a freshman. He was very athletic and exercised daily. Soccer practice was pretty intense, and he really enjoyed and appreciated what his coach put them through to prepare them for game day.

His mother had a membership at the YMCA, and when he was two years old he began taking swimming lessons. They spent a lot of time at the YMCA, and it became natural for him to know that working out his body was a way to demonstrate gratitude for his health.

As Joel got older, sometimes they would work out together at the YMCA, and he really respected his mother's healthy lifestyle and disciplined approach to her body and her health. They always led a very active lifestyle.

She had only stopped working out when she began to get really sick, but she always told him that she would get well soon and start exercising again. She reminded him that she was the one who was sick, and that he needed to stay active. She joked that she would not want to embarrass him by kicking his butt when they worked out together again.

Joel only prayed that she would soon be better and that they could go back to doing the things they loved. He would always be there for his mom and be the positive man that she wanted for him to be.

She always challenged Joel to use his imagination. She wanted him to be creative and imaginative, and that was why he was always so involved in so many school projects. He always spoke up and participated, offering new ideas.

Joel was not shy, because he was never afraid to speak up, and had little concern about what people would think or say about his ideas. His mother had told him many times that it was human nature for people to always offer criticism, especially unwanted criticism, and that he should never care what anyone thought him or said about him.

His mother said that as long as his actions did not offend the laws of God or the laws of men, he should never be concerned about what people said about him. He should only care what God would think about him.

It was amazing for him to realize that each of his father's missives carried a principle that had been planted in his mind by his mother years before. Over time, the ideas had become habits that truly defined who he was meant to be.

Since early childhood, he had formed the habit of getting up early and preparing for his day. He would sometimes arrive at school long before anyone was there, and would run around the school track at least five miles every day.

His friends thought he was crazy because he never slept in, and Joel would tell them that people who slept too much lost extra hours and days of their life that they could be making useful. Joel told them that people slept too much because they did not know what to do with their waking hours. They did not have personal goals in life.

There had been so many different young men that he had considered friends, but who really were not. They found him overly mature and didn't like the way he thought about life. They told him that he didn't know how to have fun and enjoy life, but it was they who were wrong about how life should be enjoyed.

He still remembered the day that one of his friends invited him to skip school with him and smoke pot. He was almost 14 years old, and by that time his mother had had a conversation with him about all sorts of drugs.

His mother had told Joel that she was not always going to be at his side, and that one day he would have to make a choice about drugs. She said that she only hoped that he would be strong enough to walk away and say no to drugs.

When Joel turned his friend down, he began to pressure Joel, and Joel got a bit frustrated with his friend. Joel told him that he wanted nothing to do with drugs, and that his friend should also stay away from drugs. He said that if he was going to keep pressuring him, he did not want him as a friend anymore. Needless to say, that was the last time that his so-called friend ever spoke to him.

He had been a very healthy child, but he did get sick a couple of times during his childhood with ear or throat infections. His mother gave him the antibiotics that the doctor recommended, but he never took any other type of medication.

Joel had always felt such gratitude to God for all of the blessings he had been given him in life, but now he appreciated his parents more than ever. He loved his mother so much, and yearned to meet his father.

Although he was concerned about his mother's health, he had faith in God that she would overcome the cancer that threatened her life. He stayed positive and learned to worry only about the things that he could control. He put his focus on enjoying her presence one day at a time.

He had so many wonderful memories from his past birthdays, but this one was going to surpass all of them by far. He had received one of the best gifts that he could have asked for. Now that God had brought his father into his life, he wanted him to stay. He wanted to meet him and know him.

He grabbed his father's photo and stared at it before he said, "Dad, I can't wait to meet you, to know you. I know that one day you and I will sit together and talk, and until that day comes I pray that God will protect and bless you always." He lay on the bed as he held the picture, and smiled at the idea of what was soon to come. He closed his eyes and pictured the encounter. Soon he would meet his father, and his life would be complete.

Thirteen

Joel gently knocked on the door to his mother's bedroom, then heard her delicate voice inviting him to come in.

He reached for the light switch and turned on the lamp on the night stand next to his mother's bed. The dark room was instantly illuminated.

She was lying in bed as he walked in. She slowly lifted herself, fluffed up the pillow and placed it behind her back as she sat up. She looked at Joel and smiled, rubbing her eyes. Her smile was so beautiful as she invited him to sit next to her on the bed.

"Good morning, Joel, what time is it?"

"Good morning, Mom. It's almost 4:30 in the morning." He smiled at her.

"Are you okay, son?"

"I feel wonderful, Mom; thanks. How do you feel?"

"I feel okay, Joel. A little bit tired, but nothing I can't handle." She winked at him with a smile.

"Did you get any sleep, Joel?" She smiled at him.

"I got plenty of sleep, Mom. I'm just ready to get this wonderful day started. Mom I want to invite you to take a drive with me. Are you up for it?"

"Are you kidding, Joel? You know how I feel about these unexpected drives. I'd love to; just give me a few minutes to take a shower and I'll join you."

Joel waited for his mother to get ready. As soon as she was dressed she came out into the living room where Joel was sitting on the couch. As soon as he saw her, he went to her, putting his right arm in her left and escorting her out of the house.

They were blessed to live in San Diego, only about 20 minutes away from the beach. He held the car door open for her and helped her get in the car. He wanted to make sure that she was okay. Gently he closed the door, then hurried to the driver's side and got in.

He glanced at his mom and smiled as he started the car. He turned on the radio and her favorite music began playing. She loved most of the music from the 80s, and since Joel had grown up listening to that music, he grew to love it as well. Before she got sick, he had downloaded all of her favorite music to an iPod that he had bought for her birthday. She had been so happy when he gave it to her.

She used her iPod all of the time, but especially when she worked out or did chores at home. It had been a few weeks since his mother had played her favorite songs, and Joel knew how she felt about music. She always said that music was food for the soul, and that it could instantly make anyone happy. Joel wanted to see his mother smiling and happy.

The song by the Cars, "Drive," was playing. She smiled at him and said, "Turn it up, son; I love this song." He already knew that, since she would always say that whenever her favorite song was playing. She had so many favorites. He smiled back at her as he turned the volume up for her. He knew that she really liked that song, because she used to play it over and over.

When the song was over, Joel turned down the volume and asked her, "Why do you like that song so much, Mom?" He already knew the answer because she had told him, but he loved watching the expression on her face when she shared memories of better times.

"Your dad used to play this song all the time, and it was the first song he played for me," she said, smiling. "Every time I hear this song, it reminds me of your dad. It takes me back to those times when I felt so much love and happiness with your dad."

"That's great, Mom," Joel responded, remembering that it was the song that his father had played when she first went out with him.

He glanced at her and realized that she did look a little bit better than the day before. He couldn't wait to see her well again. She had had her last surgery only a month earlier, and he could see that she was slowly getting better. All she needed was to be declared "cancer-free" by her doctor.

He turned the volume up again and drove in silence, letting her enjoy her favorite music. He imagined that each of her favorite songs brought wonderful memories back to her. He loved doing little things for his mother that would make her happy, and she had always loved music, all sorts of music.

She used to tell Joel that when she was pregnant with him, she would always play music and talk to him about each song and how she felt about it. She would joke that she was surprised that he wasn't born singing.

Ever since he was a small child, she would always play music whenever he was home with her on weekends helping with the chores. She would always remind him that listening to music did wonders for the spirit and the mind.

When they arrived at one of their favorite beaches, Joel parked on the side of the road facing the ocean. They were only a few feet away from the sand. The sun was barely rising, and that was exactly what he wanted to experience with his mother. There were a few surfers already in the water, but for the most part, they had the beach to themselves.

He shut off the engine and hurried to the passenger side to open the door for his mother. He helped her out of the car and again took her by the arm, as he always had since he was a child. They slowly walked a few steps toward the beach.

The shoreline lit up with a sunrise-gold glow. Streams of light showered the dreamy sea. The limitless sky gazed down upon the golden beach as sheets of light lit up the sea with their glow.

He took her to one of their favorite spots, and they both sat on the sand. Joel could see as the sun slowly peeked over the horizon. The view was breathtaking as the sun rose behind the waves to the east, making its slow journey across the sky.

It was almost magical to look at the edge and see how the sky changed from blood-red to orange, pink, purple, and then blue as the sun came up. He could also see the rays breaking through the clouds. The waves were creasing and swirling in the tranquil sea. The horizon seemed to be stitched with a gold line. The sea was sparking its own symphony.

He turned and faced his mother as he listened to the sounds around them. They were so close to the water that he could hear the sound of the waves and he feel the air around them beginning to warm up. The waves were rippling onto the feather-soft sand. It was something amazing to experience, and he had seen it many times with his mom and by himself throughout his life. He knew that she really enjoyed it.

She had taken Joel to witness a sunrise for the very first time on his sixth birthday. She wanted to talk him about the wonders of getting up early. Since the age of six, Joel had established a habit of getting up early and starting his day without ever having to rush. He had witnessed the sunrise many times since that birthday, and would always think of his mother any time she was not with him.

"Thanks for bringing me here today, Joel. I really needed this," she said as she reached for his chin with her right hand and caressed it.

"Thanks for coming with me, Mom. I really appreciate it and I've been wanting to do this, but I wanted to wait for the right moment. That moment was today, right now."

"I love the beach, son, and having the opportunity to watch the sunrise is so magical. You know how I've always felt about it."

"Yes of course I do, Mom. I'll never forget our conversation when I turned six. I wanted to bring you here where it's so peaceful and beautiful to talk to you about my father and the letters you gave me last night."

"Why am I not surprised that you want to talk to me about your father? Did you read any of his letters, son?" she asked as she closed her eyes and sighed.

"Did I read any of his letters, Mom? I read all of his letters, many times over last night," he said with his chin high and a gleam in his eyes.

"Are you okay, son?" she asked, biting her lower lip.

"Why wouldn't I be okay, if I was raised by the best mother in the world, who prepared me from the time I was a small child to deal with life and face any challenges I would encounter? It was you who taught me that every experience comes to teach us a lesson that we need to learn so that we can rise to the next level in our life, and I understand how this will prepare me for the next lesson," Joel said sincerely, sensing how important it was for his mother.

"I'm so proud of you, Joel, and so glad that you truly understand that," she said quietly, her eyes darting up to the sky.

"I have to tell you, Mom, that learning that my father is alive and that I'm truly a result of who he is, makes me very happy," he said with a satisfied smile.

"I'm so glad to hear that, Joel. Although your father has been gone most of your life, he's has been here the whole time. His teachings have made me the woman that I am today, and I'll always be grateful for that. His letters inspired me and motivated me to keep going, to never give up, to learn to love and accept my life, but also to have faith in God to make the best of my life despite my circumstances." She shifted her gaze back to Joel.

"I just can't believe that all of these years, while I was growing up wondering who my father was, he was in prison. I would never in a million years have guessed that. But I'm just really grateful to him that he didn't give up on us either, and that he was there for us in the best and only possible way that he knew."

"You father was actually a great man, and I see so much of him in you, not just physically, but also in your humility, your sense of humor, the way you carry yourself. Your father was a very loving man who cared immensely about his family, and he cared the most about you, Joel," she said with a shy smile.

"Mom, do you still love my father?" Joel asked, feeling solace in knowing that his father really did love him.

"Of course I still love him. When I married him I swore to God that only death would separate us, and I meant what I said when I promised him that at the altar."

"Most women would have already moved on and found themselves someone else."

"I'm not like most women, son. I'm not judging anyone, Joel, but it's sad that people don't take their vows seriously when they get married. People find it easier to get a divorce, break up a family, than to stand together and fight for their family and loved ones and keep the vows they made to each other. It's as if they never took those vows seriously. They don't fight to save and protect the most important thing in life, which is family."

"I always knew that you were special, Mom, but I never realized just what a wonderful human being you truly are," Joel said as he took a deep breath.

"I don't feel special, son, but thank you for your kind words. You may call me old-fashioned, but I could never be with anyone but your father. I believe that in order for you to have physical contact with someone else, there needs to be a very special bond called love, because if not, you are just like animals mating."

"But Mom, you sacrificed the best years of your life being by yourself, and my father is serving a life sentence," he said as he gently scratched his jaw.

"I'm okay with that, son. I never saw it as a sacrifice. Being physically intimate with a man I didn't love would have been a true sacrifice for me. I have no interest in having another man in my life. I've led a very happy and complete life, Joel. I wouldn't have it any other way," she said with determination.

"I believe you, Mom, and it's admirable that you think that way."

"Joel, I want to ask you what you're going to do now that you know your father is alive. Are you going to write back to him? Are you going to allow him into your life?" she asked, licking her lip with cautious hope.

"I already wrote back to him last night. I'll mail the letter out on Monday, and yes, I do want to be part of his life. He actually sent me a visitor's application that I had to fill out to be approved to visit him. I really want to see him," he responded, looking straight into her eyes.

"I'm so glad to know that you've decided to be part of your father's life and that you'll be visiting him."

"How about you? Will you be visiting him?"

"Not right now, son. I really don't want your father to see me this way. I know that I'll get better, and once I beat this cancer, I'll visit him too. He sent me an application too, and I'll send it back sometime soon, but I really don't want him to see me this way. But now I'll write back to him as well."

"I'm so happy, Mom. You have no idea what this all means to me. I know that you'll get better soon, and we can both go visit my father."

"Joel, I want you to do me a favor," she said as she leaned forward.

"Yes, Mom, anything you need," he responded with a deep gratifying sigh.

"Now that you know that everything you've learned that has helped you become the man you are today is due mainly to your father's teachings, will you share those principles with as many people as possible?"

"You want me to teach people about Dad's principles?"

"Yes, son."

"You know, Mom, in one of my father's letters he mentions that if he was a free man he would give back to others, and that he would give his time and work with kids my age who are living lives with very little direction. I think doing something like that would be pretty awesome. I'd love to inspire other kids my age to learn to live a better life, to give value to the things in life that truly matter, and to be happy in general."

"Yes, that's what I mean, Joel. Help others be the very best version of themselves, and you'll find your success."

"Mom, I promise you that I'll think of a way to do something like that and help others, and I know that's important for you, but for now I need to focus my time and energy on two other things that matter more. The first one is you, and the second is establishing a relationship with my father. Once I've taken care of those two things, I'll focus my time and energy on what you've asked me to do. Is that fair, Mom?"

"Of course it is, son. I'm so proud of you. Thanks for being such a great son and for bringing me to my favorite place by the ocean."

"I wouldn't have it any other way, Mom. I'm very blessed to have such an extraordinary woman as a mother. I promise you, Mom, that I'll do the impossible to never let you down." Joel leaned over and placed a gentle kiss on his mother's cheek.

"Joel, your father was always a huge inspiration for me in so many ways, even since the beginning," she said quietly.

"What do you mean, Mom?" he said, looking out into the ocean.

"Joel, I had a really troubled childhood, because I was raised by foster parents. When my parents died in a car accident when I was little, no one from either side of the family took me in. I was only three years old when they died, so I really don't have any memories of them. I went from foster home to foster home. I wasn't a victim of abuse or anything like that, but I never felt wanted or loved, and that made me very insecure," she said, with a tense expression on her face.

"I didn't know that, Mom; I'm sorry. I knew that you were an orphan, but you never really spoke about your childhood."

"When I was a teenager, I was very depressed, and I found comfort in food and gained a lot of weight. If I was sad or depressed, I would eat anything I wanted. When I first met your dad, it was very difficult for me to believe that such a handsome man would even look at me, because I was overweight." She hunched her shoulders as she spoke.

"I thought you were always very disciplined with your diet, Mom."

"When I started dating your dad, he had a way of getting people motivated, and he encouraged me to start working out and taught me about eating the right foods. He did it with such charm that it didn't offend me, but inspired me to love myself and take better care of my health and my body. Your father was always eating healthy and he always worked out. It was he who taught me that, and in a matter of months, after I changed my diet and started exercising regularly, I lost the weight and I've kept it off ever since," she said with a deep breath.

"I had no idea, Mom. I've always seen the discipline that you have and nothing else. I'm so proud of you," he said, parting his lips.

"For years after your father was locked up, I almost lost my discipline and wanted to find comfort in food again. It was really tough for me, but I didn't give in. I have to tell you that every missive that your father wrote for you helped me in so many different ways in my life. Those missives helped me become a better person," she said, crossing her arms. "There was a time in my life where I almost lost my faith in everything, son."

"You've always been such a great example for me, Mom, and your faith has been very important to you," he said, leaning closer.

"You were never exposed to any of those moments in my life, Joel, because you were little and I didn't want to share that with you, but for a while in my life, I didn't believe in anything. I was too angry, too resentful. Why am I sharing this with you? Because I want you to know that we all go through very difficult times in life. It's when we're facing adversity that we must make the right choices in life, and that's when our true character is revealed. I was afraid, angry, resentful, and bitter before I met your father, and I experienced the same negative emotions when he was arrested. I faced those same emotions all over again because I felt so alone," she said, furrowing her eyebrows.

"You overcame them, Mom," he said with a gleam in his eyes.

"Son, all of us can either give up on life or just keep on trying. There were moments in my life when I doubted everything I was doing, but over time, as I received each of your father's missives, I grew wiser and learned to truly appreciate life, to be grateful for the things I had and not think only about the things I wanted. I found my faith again and never let it go. I made faith my best friend, my companion, my everything. Son, anyone can change their life, their circumstances for the better if they just choose to do that. It might seem as if I've always been very stable in every aspect of my life, but that's not the case. I'm as human as anyone else and have made mistakes, but I've also learned from them," she said, rubbing the back of her neck.

"I'm so proud of you. You've endured so much and yet you never gave up," Joel said, giving his mother a tender look.

"I owe your father so much more than you imagine, Joel, and I thank God every moment for the challenges in life that I've had to face. My faith in God won't let me fall or collapse. All of my challenges have made me into the woman I am today. I'm going to keep leaning on our God always, son," she said, smiling.

His mother took his hand and held it as she looked out at the ocean, smiling. Her countenance was one of joy, hope, and serenity. Joel felt so peaceful sitting next to her, and he prayed that God would allow his mom to be healthy and happy again. She deserved great things in life, to be happy, but he knew that she would be content with just being healthy again.

Joel felt God's presence in that precise moment, as he saw the beauty of the ocean and the purity in his mother's smile and warm gaze. The blanket of paradise-blue sky was fringed with clouds. He thanked God for the moment they were sharing and for everything he had in life. He felt so alive as the warm breeze stroked his face, the sunbeams warmed their bodies and their souls, and the smell of the ocean rose from the steaming seaweed.

Great things were coming. He felt it; really good things would soon arrive. The ocean was calm and serene, and for the first time in a long time Joel felt that his feelings resembled those of the ocean. Just as he had had the opportunity to experience another magical sunrise with his mother, he had faith that one day he would have the opportunity to share a sunset with the man that he now knew as his father.

He was still and knew that God was there; God was everywhere. He stared at the ocean and contemplated true purity, and in silence he thanked God for allowing him to share such a good conversation with his mother. There are no words to describe the language that silence brings. It has been said that silence is God's language and everything else is merely a translation.

He knew that everyone was born with a purpose in life, and he understood his life's purpose at that moment. He had so much to learn, and he wanted to grow as a son, but more importantly as a human being. He had no idea where he would end up, but he knew for certain that he was doing what God expected of him. He feared nothing and chose to face his next test as if through the eyes of a child, without fear and full of love and passion. A new chapter would soon start, and Joel waited anxiously to turn the page and begin his next lesson.

Fourteen

As Joel waited to meet with the doctor, he thought back to the year before when he had found out about his mother's diagnosis. Joel had no idea what it really meant when he was told that his mother had breast cancer. The only thing he did know was that he wanted to understand and learn as much he could about it, so he set out to read and research as much as he could.

He wanted to support his mother and help her get through the experience. He wanted to make sure that he was prepared to face this new lesson that life was giving him. He soon found out that breast cancer had no respect for anyone. It did not care about who you were, your age, color, where you came from, or how rich or poor you were.

His mother had been diagnosed with stage 3C breast cancer. Through his research, Joel learned that stage 3C breast cancer meant that the cancer had extended beyond the immediate region of the tumor and might have invaded nearby lymph nodes and muscles, but had not spread to distant organs.

After his mother had told him about her diagnosis, Joel had asked her to let him come with her to her next doctor's visit. He wanted to understand more and ask questions that might help him help his mother. He wanted to know and understand what his mother was really facing and what he was up against. She was supposed to meet with her doctor to discuss her surgery options and prepare for surgery if she agreed.

The pathologist had spoken with both of them and had explained the surgery process. In order to remove all of the cancer, he would have to perform a sentinel lymph node biopsy. The sentinel lymph node is the first lymph node where the cancer is likely to spread.

The process would require them to inject a radioactive substance near the tumor, and the substance would then flow through the lymph ducts to the lymph nodes. Once the first lymph node received the substance, it would be removed. The pathologist would then view the lymph node tissue under a microscope to look for cancer cells. After the sentinel lymph node biopsy, the surgeon would remove the tumor by performing a breast-conserving surgery.

He explained that if cancer cells were not found in the sentinel lymph node, it might not be necessary to remove more lymph nodes. If cancer cells were found in the sentinel lymph node, more lymph nodes would be removed through a separate incision, using a procedure called lymph node dissection.

Because of the tumor's size and the fact that it was found in three of the 15 lymph nodes they had removed from her arm, his mother had already been having chemotherapy to help shrink the tumor.

She had been receiving chemotherapy for three months. Joel would go with his mother every time, and afterwards, he witnessed how she kept vomiting. As much of a warrior as she was, though she tried to remain strong, after each treatment she would get extremely exhausted and weak.

They both knew from the doctor that these were all side effects of chemotherapy. They had talked about it before she started chemotherapy and had prepared themselves mentally, but Joel soon realized that no human being could ever be fully prepared for chemotherapy sessions. He wished with all his heart that he could trade places with his mother. It really hurt him to see her go through that.

Joel thought back about when his mother began to lose her hair, and had decided to just cut it off and shave her head. He thought she was going to be heartbroken because she had to cut her long beautiful black hair, but she just joked about not having to worry about having a bad hair day.

He knew that his mother was a strong woman, but he hadn't realized just how strong she was until he saw her dealing with her condition, always keeping her chin up, smiling and talking to him about faith and God.

Joel would come home sometimes and see how his mother barely had the energy to get out of bed. He could see how she strove to do the impossible so that Joel could see her in as normal a state as possible. They would take walks almost every day, and although she didn't say anything or complain, Joel knew that his mother dreaded having to go to the chemotherapy sessions.

Her chemo treatments had now been going on for a year, followed by radiation and several surgeries. She was now receiving post-cancer treatments, and Joel had a lot of faith that she would defeat this terrible disease.

When his mother had told him about her breast cancer, Joel had felt as if his heart was shattering. At first, he was afraid for his mother and what the future would hold, but with her continued optimism, he was able to be more supportive of her and focus more on how he could help her rather than worrying.

Ever since he was 14 his mother had talked to him about worry, how to manage it, and how he should never worry about things that he could not control. Joel had understood that principle years before, but having to face his mother's breast cancer diagnosis made him veer a little off course. His mother was quick to remind him again not to worry, but instead to focus on what he could do to help her, so that was what he had been doing.

He and his mother visited her doctor two weeks after Joel's 18th birthday. He had waited with great anticipation to hear that she was "cancer-free," and he wanted to see that all of that fighting, pushing, and determination had defeated the cancer and that she could go back to living a normal life.

His mother was sitting next to Joel in the doctor's office, and she held his hand as the doctor walked in and reviewed her original diagnosis, treatment, progress and current diagnosis.

He sat directly in front of them as he studied her medical chart, then put the chart down as he shifted his gaze to her.

He smiled as he said, "Congratulations, Alexia, you have beaten the cancer. You are cancer-free." His mother dropped his hand and rushed to the doctor to give him a hug. She quickly released him as she pressed her fingers to her smiling lips.

"Thank you, Dr. Smith, for everything that you did to help me, and for your patience and support." Her voice was full of emotion.

"You're welcome, and thank you for being such a trooper. I've met so many wonderful people who have endured what you have, and most of them are such strong people, real warriors, but I've never met anyone like you."

"What do you mean, Dr. Smith?"

"You're very strong, like most of my patients, and showed a lot of courage. But you also have such a vibrant spirit, full of optimism and love, and that, my dear, makes you pretty unique. It never allowed you to become negative about your circumstances. I've just never witnessed anything like that. I was also fortunate enough to hear many of your conversations with other patients. You're a true inspiration for many to follow."

"Aren't we put in this world to help and inspire one another, Dr. Smith?"

"Yes, of course, but you took it to the next level. Although you were enduring your own pain, every time you came in for chemotherapy treatments, before your session, you would sit and talk to many of the patients and encourage them to have faith, to never give up on themselves or life. I just found that admirable," he said, smiling warmly at her.

"Thank you, Dr. Smith. If you must know, what really kept me going every day and didn't allow me to give up was my faith. I really believed that I was meant to do the best that I could under my circumstances, but that ultimately God would have the last word, and that's just what I did."

"Most of my patients always worried about one thing or another, but you never showed any signs of worry, which I commend you for. It's very unusual to see that."

"Worrying only makes you sicker, and it does nothing to improve the situation. I only worry about the things that are within my control, and even then I do my best not to allow worry into my mind."

"I'm very happy for you, and to see that you've beaten the cancer. I'm sure that you're probably relieved to be finished with the demands of the treatments and that you're ready to put the experience behind you, but please remember to continue with the post-cancer treatments."

"Yes, I'll follow your instructions, Dr. Smith."

"Make sure that you start the follow-up cancer care plan. I'm going to give you some information to read to prepare you for going back to your normal life. Expect to visit your doctor every four months for the next two years. When you visit the doctor, they will look for side effects from the treatment you received and also check to make sure the cancer hasn't returned."

"I'll read the information you're giving me, Dr. Smith."

"You may also want your doctor to help you set up a wellness plan that will include ways you can take care of your physical, emotional, social, and even spiritual needs. There's a lot of help out there for survivors like you, but I have a feeling that while at first you may be attending support groups, you're going to ultimately end up leading those groups." He smiled broadly.

"Dr. Smith, thank you again for everything you've done and are still doing for me."

Joel got up and walked over to Dr. Smith and shook his hand as he said, "Thank you, Dr. Smith for everything you've done for my mom, and for spending time with me educating me about this disease and my mom's treatments. You were always there to answer all of my questions, and that really helped prepare me better to help my mom get through this."

"You're welcome, Joel. You're a fine young man, and I can see that you've had a great upbringing. I can see where you get it from. You should be very proud of your mom," Dr. Smith said as he faced Joel.

"I'm very proud of my mom, for more reasons that you can ever imagine." Joel smiled as he firmly shook the doctor's hand.

Joel promised Dr. Smith that he was going to be very involved in supporting breast cancer research, but more importantly in sharing with others and educating them about the disease. His mother also promised that she was going to be very involved in helping others who were facing or dealing with cancer.

Joel and his mother walked out of Dr. Smith's office and smiled at each other. They walked together in silence, both immersed in their own thoughts. One thing was certain: they had a lot to be grateful for. Joel knew that his mother would expect them to give gratitude to God, but knowing her, she would find a way to demonstrate her gratitude, and that would be by helping someone in need.

They had both been anxiously waiting for this moment. Now that his mother had been declared cancer-free, they would go back to their normal life, but now they were prepared to face anything. They had both been presented with a difficult lesson, and had overcome it.

They had gained the wisdom and courage to face any other lesson life might throw their way. Now Joel understood that life could bring pain, but that it was up to them to turn the pain into bliss.

Joel stopped and turned to face his mother, looked her in the eyes, then held her gently. He was so happy to know that she had beaten cancer.

He gently released her and said, "Mom, I'm so happy for you. You were right all those times that you reminded me that I needed to have more faith than ever. Even though I did have faith, I'd be lying to you if I didn't tell you that sometimes fear defeated my faith."

"I understand, son. I'm just glad that you overcame your fears and held on to your faith. God is great, and knowing that he's here for us is what will keep each of us going. In spite of your dad's circumstances, he has always maintained his faith."

"I know, Mom, but I just want you to know that there's so much I want to do to educate and support all cancer victims."

"You'll soon have the opportunity to show God your gratitude, just like I will also demonstrate my gratitude. Let's go home, Joel, and start our new life."

"Okay, Mom. Let's go home. Now I understand that saying, "What doesn't kill you will make you stronger."

His mother took Joel's arm, and he led her out of the clinic.

Fifteen

Joel had received another letter from his father a week earlier. That letter was very different than all his other missives. He wanted to let him know that both of their visitor applications had been approved, and that they could visit him any time they chose.

He gave Joel some more information about visiting days and hours. They could visit him from 8:00 a.m. until 3:00 p.m. on Thursday, Friday, Saturday or Sunday.

It had been six months since Joel's 18th birthday, the day that he had found out about his father. So much had happened since then, and Joel had been anxiously waiting to hear that their visitor applications had been approved.

Shortly after receiving his father's letter telling him that they could visit, Joel decided that he wanted to have a better understanding of where his father was being kept. He researched as much as he could about the maximum security prison that his father called home.

ADX, also known as the "Alcatraz of the Rockies," was the U.S. Penitentiary in Florence, Colorado that housed the worst criminals in America's vast prison network. These were male inmates in the federal prison system who had been deemed the most dangerous and in need of the strictest control. ADX opened in November 1994. It was documented that the residents of Fremont County welcomed the prison as a source of employment.

The Florence Federal Correctional Complex is operated by the Federal Bureau of Prisons (BOP), a division of the United States Department of Justice. ADX also includes an adjacent minimum-security camp that as of 2014 houses more prisoners than the supermax unit.

Heavily armed patrols cruise the extensive complex, and at least a dozen daunting gun towers rise above squat brick buildings. Walls topped with razor wire partially block the Colorado mountains.

The inmates spend as many as 23 hours a day alone in a 7 by 12-foot concrete cell. All meals are slid through slots in the doors. The bed is composed of a concrete slab covered with a thin mattress and some blankets.

The prisoners are allowed some access to natural light through a single window about 42 inches high and 4 inches wide, but they are not able to see past the building. Each cell has a desk made of concrete with immovable stools. Very solid walls prevent prisoners from seeing other cells or having any form of contact with other inmates.

From their cells, inmates can never view the sky, and have very little contact with the outside guards or any other prison staff.

Any time they leave their cells, they must wear leg irons, handcuffs and stomach chains while being escorted by the prison guards.

Each prisoner is permitted one hour a day of recreation in an outdoor cage that is a bit larger than their prison cell. Once inside the cage, the inmate can glimpse the sky.

Joel could not understand how men could be so destructive to one another. If his father had been charged with drug distribution, why was he serving time in a prison that housed the most violent inmates: disruptive gang leaders, spies, and killers as well as convicted terrorists? It made no sense for his father to be serving a life sentence in that place.

He wanted to make sure that his mother was well aware of where his father was serving his sentence. He didn't want her to get upset once she understood where he was, but knowing his mother, she probably knew everything.

How was it possible for his father to be as positive as he was about life and to have acquired so much wisdom in a place where it was clearly very easy to lose his mind? Being in an environment where there is only isolation, with no direct, unrestrained contact with other human beings, would surely leave inmates with a fundamental loss of even basic social skills and adaptive behaviors.

He could see how it would be easy for many of these prisoners to feel somewhat paranoid about the intentions of other inmates. Joel could only imagine what his father had been exposed to. He was amazed that his father was who he was, and he wanted to research his case and get as involved as he could to help his father get out of there.

He had to remain strong for his parents, but realized that his father's situation was much worse than anything he could have ever imagined. He had no idea that men could do that to other men. It was just so inhumane.

Joel remembered that his father had told him in one of his missives that in the place where he found himself, you either went crazy or grew wise. He was glad that his father had learned to adapt and to make the best of his circumstances, and had full control of his mind.

He had shared that many times he had traveled to different parts of the world through the books he read and the thoughts he allowed into his mind, without ever stepping out of his prison cell.

Joel and his mother had already discussed their plans for visiting. They would have to fly from San Diego to Salt Lake City, and from there they would take another plane to Colorado Springs, where they would rent a car to drive to Florence, Colorado.

At first they had discussed the possibility of driving to Colorado, but then they realized that the drive was very long and that they would lose a lot of time on the road, so they opted to fly instead. They would much rather spend more time visiting with his father than on the road driving.

They had so much to talk to his father about and so much catching up to do. Joel couldn't wait to see him and talk to him. He thought about his father sitting inside that cell year after year, and couldn't help but feel an indescribable sadness in his heart.

His father had shared such wisdom, even as he was locked inside a living hell, that Joel couldn't help but respect him and who he was. Despite everything that he had gone through, he was still standing, not allowing his circumstances to bring him down.

Joel smiled at the thought of seeing his father for the first time. He appreciated the silence around him as he stared into space and said, "See you soon, Dad." Then he walked over to speak with his mother.

Sixteen

A month after receiving his father's letter telling them that they had been approved to visit, Joel had bought the airline tickets. The day that they would be flying to see his father, Joel was so excited that he had already checked them in online and printed their boarding passes. Now he was waiting for his mother to join him to drive to the San Diego airport.

He wanted to see his father, to speak with him. There were so many questions that remained unanswered, and so many different thoughts flowed through his mind. He knew that he wasn't angry at his father and didn't harbor any resentment. He just wanted to know so much about him, to understand everything better, and to do everything possible to help him.

His mother had recovered so much in the last few months that she was back to her normal self. She wanted to do so much to help people who were facing cancer by being there for them and their families. She had been actively participating in support groups for the last two months, and she told Joel that it helped her more than the people she was trying to help.

She always came home wanting to share stories about people she had met who were dealing with cancer, and wanted nothing more than to help them get through that difficult time in their lives. She met many cancer survivors with amazing stories who were giving back by volunteering and counseling people with cancer. She always said that she knew that she couldn't change the world alone, but that she would do her part. Helping people made her so happy.

She had said to him, "Joel, do you know that we were all born to serve one another?"

"Of course, Mom. You taught me that at an early age," he responded with a satisfied smile.

"There's no greater satisfaction than being able to serve and help others, son. I feel the happiest when I know that I've said or done something to make someone else happy." She was beaming as she said this, and Joel couldn't help but smile tenderly back at her.

"I can see that, Mom."

"I've come to realize, son, that true fulfillment comes only from helping others, and we are more blessed when we give than when we receive. You should never underestimate the difference you can make in the lives of others, Joel," she said in a steady, lower-pitched voice. She always managed to remind him how blessed he truly was.

The day before, Joel had received another letter from his father. He wanted to make sure they had received the previous letter and that they knew that they could go visit him.

His father told Joel that he wanted him and his mother to know that he still had hope and faith that he would soon be released, even though he was serving a life sentence.

He shared with Joel that he had been diligently researching anything he could find about any possible amendments Congress might pass that would affect his sentencing.

It had been only a few years since he had come across FAMM (Families Against Mandatory Minimums), a nonprofit, nonpartisan organization fighting for smart sentencing laws that protect public safety. He attached a copy of an article he had about FAMM that discussed in detail how they were founded, who they were and how they had helped many inmates.

FAMM is supported by taxpayers, families, prisoners, law enforcement, attorneys, judges, criminal justice experts and concerned citizens.

FAMM advocates for sensible state and federal sentencing reform and helps lessen the burden of overcrowded prisons on taxpayers, shift resources from excessive incarceration to law enforcement and other programs proven to reduce crime and recidivism, and mobilize those lives harmed by unfair prison sentences to work constructively for change.

FAMM was founded by Julie Stewart. In 1990, Julie, who was a public affairs director at the Cato Institute, first learned about mandatory minimum sentencing laws. Her brother had been arrested for growing marijuana in Washington State, and had plead guilty. Even though it was his first offense, he had been sentenced to five years in a federal prison without parole.

The judge criticized the punishment as too harsh, but the mandatory minimum law left him no choice. Motivated by her own family's experience, Julie created Families Against Mandatory Minimum (FAMM) in 1991. Though her brother had long since left prison, had a beautiful family and a good job, Julie continued to lead FAMM in the fight for punishment that fit the crime and the offender.

Since FAMM's first meeting in 1991, the organization has grown to include 70,000 supporters, including prisoners, family members, practitioners and concerned citizens.

When Joel's father found out about FAMM, he became a member and also educated other prisoners about it. He told other prisoners that there were too many drug offenders still behind bars, serving lengthy sentences that didn't fit the crimes. He had been sentenced to life for a non-violent drug offense 18 years earlier. He felt that he was a great candidate for having his sentence shortened and had been participating as much as he was able.

He told Joel that he wanted to share what was currently happening so that he would have a better understanding of it.

Attached to the letter and the copy of the article, he also received a separate typed piece of paper from his father. The paper said that the U.S. Sentencing Commission had sent Congress eight amendments to the federal sentencing guidelines. Among the recommended guideline changes was one that would lower all drug sentencing by two levels. FAMM referred to that amendment as "Drugs Minus Two." That change could lower the sentencing guidelines for drug offenses by an average of 11 months per defendant.

There were three important dates coming up that Joel needed to remember. On June 10, 2014, the U.S. Sentencing Commission would be holding a hearing on whether to make retroactive the proposed amendment to lower the drug tables by two levels (Drugs Minus Two).

FAMM testified at the hearing that led to the new amendment. They recommended that the Commission invite former prisoners who had benefitted when they made "Crack Minus Two" retroactive in 2007, so they could see what a difference retroactivity had made in people's lives.

Friends and family members of prisoners were encouraged to send letters to the Commission in support of "Drugs Minus Two" by July 7th. On July 18th, the Commission would vote on whether to make "Drugs Minus Two" retroactive. FAMM was pulling out all of the stops to persuade the Commission to do the right thing and make the guideline change retroactive.

On July 18, 2014, the U.S. Sentencing Commission voted unanimously to apply Amendment 728, which downwardly adjusted the Sentencing Commission's Drug Quantity Table by two levels retroactively, so that it applies to cases finalized before its enactment. The retroactive application of the "Drug Minus Two" amendments would go in effect on November 1, 2014. However, pursuant to the Commission's directive, no person would be released under the retroactive application of the amendment until November 1, 2015.

The retroactive amendment represents a watershed moment in federal drug sentencing that will likely bring relief to tens of thousands of federal prisoners.

Joel placed the piece of paper on the kitchen table as he ran his hand through his hair. He had read the same letter several times since he had received it the day before. He still could not believe what he was reading. He felt a floating sensation, as if all his burdens had been lifted. His father could actually be released from prison. He clasped his hands in prayer to his lips and closed his eyes as he said, "Thank you, dear God."

When his mother had read the letter, he thought she was going to collapse. She was so happy, and couldn't stop talking about what they should do for his father, her husband, to help him with his case.

His father had told him that he had submitted an application himself, since he didn't have an attorney to represent him and didn't feel that he needed one. The process seemed rather simple but lengthy, but he had no problem waiting another year or two in the hope that he could be released from prison.

He told Joel that he had also been working with another prisoner who was serving a long sentence and could also qualify for a sentence reduction. It made him feel really good to be able to help others, and even if they denied his application and he wasn't released from prison, he would keep trying to help as many other prisoners as he could.

Joel would have to research FAMM himself to see if there was anything that he could do to increase the possibility of his father being released from prison.

Joel sat down in one of the kitchen chairs and thought about their trip. It made him feel very happy to know that their applications to visit his father had been approved, and he couldn't wait to see him. The next day, he would be meeting his father.

He was overcome with so many different emotions. He couldn't wait to see him. He went into the bathroom and splashed his face with cold water. He felt like he was dreaming, because his life had changed so much since his 18th birthday six months earlier.

He remembered what his mother had always said to him about life being composed of nothing more than moments, and if you missed the moment, then you missed your life. At that moment, he realized how right she was. It was a moment that he did not want to miss.

Just a year before, he had viewed life so differently as he struggled with seeing his mother suffer so much as she dealt with cancer. Now he had learned that every person has the ability to change the way that they see the world. A single moment could be all they need to wake them up to a new reality. He felt like he had experienced that recently.

The recent events in his life had changed everything for him. He had always prayed daily, but when he prayed now he was always asking God to give him wisdom, maturity, guidance and courage to make the right decisions in his life.

He thought about Oscar and Eddy and his conversations with them about daily prayer. They had both laughed, saying that they never prayed. He could not understand how people could wake up every day and not give thanks to God for another day of life, for their health, their family and all of the blessings they had in their life. He had daily rituals, and he prayed to God every day in the morning, in the evening and sometimes throughout the day. He would sometimes find himself praying for others.

Oscar and Eddy both told Joel that they didn't know how to pray. He told them that praying was basically having an open-hearted conversation with God, and that there was no right or wrong way to do it. It just had to be sincere and honest, and they could say whatever they felt they needed to say to God. He encouraged them to pray daily, and although they both joked about it, Joel could see that he had awakened something in his friends that that he had not seen before. He just could not imagine his life without his relationship with God.

He would continue to encourage them to find comfort and guidance in prayer. He wanted to teach them to have self-love, which would help them find peace, and eventually fill their lives with joy. He felt it was his duty to teach others about having faith, and sharing God's word was what everyone was supposed to do.

The more he focused on helping others find a spiritual life, the more he discovered himself as a human being. He felt that he was carrying a bright light and that he had to share that light. This allowed him to know himself, and other parts of himself that had been hidden away had begun to reveal themselves to him.

He had come to understand that when you acquire wisdom and maturity, you will see that everything that happens in life is an opportunity to grow, or sometimes to help heal a part of your life that needs healing. These opportunities must be seized so that you can reveal who you really are.

He was ready to go meet his father and help himself grow, learn and heal. He knew that this was another lesson, and that he would walk away having learned the greatest lesson in life. He was ready for that and so much more. Seeing his reflection in the mirror, he knew that his smile and the light in his eyes mirrored how he felt: full of joy, gratitude, and happiness.

He walked out of the bathroom and went to see if his mother needed help with her bags. They would be staying in a hotel in Florence, Colorado for three nights. They wanted to visit his father for three days in a row, taking full advantage of the trip. He knew how he felt, but he could only imagine how his mother felt; what she thought.

He took a deep breath, and with a big heartfelt smile, tapped on his mother's bedroom door. He could hear the music playing in her room. God was good; he had healed his mother and now he was giving him his father back. There was so much he had to be grateful for, and Joel knew that he would soon be giving back to help others achieve their dreams and find the peace, joy and love that he was experiencing right that moment.

Seventeen

They drove from the Colorado Springs airport into Canyon City. They were going to stay at a Best Western Hotel in Canyon City and drive into Florence, which was less than 20 minutes away from the hotel. It was an unpleasantly cold winter's night, mysterious, and the moon was sheltered by the gloomy looming clouds.

It was almost 9:00 p.m. when they left the airport. Joel was behind the wheel and was using the GPS on his phone to help guide him into Canyon City. He couldn't believe that he was this close to meeting his father.

According to the GPS, it was going to take him 50 minutes to get to Canyon City, so Joel decided to drive all the way to the hotel without stopping. There was not much traffic as they drove away from the airport.

The roads were very dark, and there were a lot of curves, so Joel had to keep his eyes on the road. He began to slow down as he drove, since he could not see very far ahead and would have little time to stop if he had to. There were signs of jumping deer on the side of the road to alert drivers that it could happen. He was happy that there were only a few vehicles on the road. He wanted to take his time and didn't want to deal with traffic.

"Are you ready to meet your father, Joel?" his mother asked, furrowing her eyebrows.

Joel had a thoughtful expression for a moment as he responded, "Yes I am, Mom."

"How about you, Mom?"

She stared thoughtfully into space before she answered, "You have no idea how long I've been waiting for this moment, son." She turned and faced Joel, giving him a meaningful look. "For years I've been thinking of this moment and wondering when it would arrive. Seeing your father again will allow me to understand so many things in my life. I need to truly come to terms with the way I feel about your father and this situation, because all this has been very difficult to me." She gasped in stunned surprise at her own admission, and for several seconds she kept silent before she said, "It doesn't mean that I don't love your father, because as I have shared with you, I'll always love him, but I need to talk to him."

"I understand what you mean, Mom. It's been 18 years since you last saw Dad, and meeting him and talking to him will help you," he said, not wanting to add to her distress.

"It's been such a long time, Joel."

"Mom, there are some things that are still unclear to me and don't make a lot of sense." Joel said, keeping his eyes on the road in front of him.

"Like what things, Joel?"

"You do understand that Dad is serving a life sentence in a prison that is known to house the most dangerous male inmates in the federal prison system, right?" Joel asked in an uncertain tone.

"Yes, I'm well aware of that, Joel." she responded, swallowing hard.

"You also know that inmates spend 23 hours of their day in small cells with no view of the outside world?"

"Yes, son, I've known that for years. Your father was transferred to ADX a few years after he was sentenced. When I first found out where he was and what his living conditions were, it broke my heart, but I couldn't allow that to bring me down, because I had you to think about. All I could do was pray for him daily, so I prayed and prayed to God to keep him safe, give him the wisdom to see his wrongdoing and repent, and the strength to endure his new life," she responded, biting her lower lip.

"You know, Mom; I don't understand how we humans can be so cruel," Joel said in a flat voice.

"You're right, son; we're even more cruel than animals. A lot of animals have demonstrated more love and compassion than a lot of humans often do," she said, crossing her arms over her chest.

"I agree, Mom. Animals don't have all the senses we have, and yet they're often less savage than we humans are. I hope my father has adapted to his life of solitude, Mom; my heart goes out to him."

"I know what you mean, son, but your father was always a very smart man and he's learned to adapt to his environment. He's found refuge in his faith in God, occupies his mind reading great books and also writes. He's managed to learn to control his mind, because in a place like that, once you lose your mind, there's no way to get it back."

"God made us so that we could learn to live with each other and love each other. We aren't meant to be living alone, even if it's inside a prison." Joel said, gently braking as he approached a curve.

"I agree with you, Joel, I find it very cruel and callous."

"What did Dad really do to end up in a place like that, Mom? Please be honest with me."

"Joel, I've been nothing but honest with you all your life. The only thing that I wasn't truthful about was that your father was alive and in a federal prison, but other than that I've always told you the truth about everything."

"I know that you have, Mom, but I just don't understand why my father is serving a life sentence and why he is in among the worst criminals."

"When your father was arrested, he was advised by his attorney to make a plea bargain deal with the District Attorney, but one of the conditions was that he needed to turn in all of the names of his business associates. Your father was only thinking of his family when he refused to accept the deal and wouldn't cooperate," she said with a heavy sigh.

"Why couldn't he have just told them who he was working with, Mom? They were criminals too, and should have paid for their crimes," Joel said, gently shaking his head.

"I agree, son, but that environment isn't what you think it is. If your father had cooperated with the District Attorney and surrendered the names of his business associates, there would have been repercussions, and not good ones."

"What sort of repercussions, Mom?"

"If he had turned in his business associates, they would have been very upset with him, and they would have found a way to hurt you, me or anyone else in his family."

"So he sacrificed his life for us?" Joel asked, gripping the steering wheel as he drove.

"Joel, I don't really believe that your father had ever imagined that he would be sentenced to life. If you think about it, the crime doesn't fit the punishment. He really thought that he would be in prison 10-15 years or so for the crime he committed, but he never thought he would be sentenced to a life term."

"I know you told me that when my dad was a little boy, he had the desire and the dream to build an empire and help his parents financially, and that it was his father who got all his children involved in selling marijuana, and that my dad just followed his father's directions. But he must have gotten involved in something much bigger than dealing marijuana," he said, wrinkling his forehead.

"It's sad to say this, son, but all your father knew and understood was that money was the most important thing in life, and according to his father's teachings, a man who had no money was not a man at all."

"My father actually believed that?" His eyes narrowed in confusion.

"He was only 12 years old when he started selling marijuana, and he loved and admired his father. He believed anything his father had to say to him or his siblings. What do you really know at that age? He saw how his father carried himself and how empowered he was, or thought he was, and all he wanted was to be just like his father."

"So my dad's dream did come true, because he built an empire?"

"Unfortunately it did, son. He got involved in something much bigger and dangerous than dealing marijuana. Your father was charged as the "leader organizer" of a methamphetamine manufacturing enterprise. He and some of his siblings and business partners were charged as co-conspirators for obtaining ephedrine, pseudoephedrine, red phosphorus and iodine from other people, and they had lab equipment to produce methamphetamine."

"That's unbelievable, Mom." He hunched his shoulders and shook his head.

"I didn't find out any of this until after your father was arrested. They leased houses under fictitious names or the names of people who weren't part of their conspiracy and hired cooks to produce the methamphetamine. Once the manufacturing process was complete, your dad and his business associates would sell the methamphetamine to other people."

"Didn't my father care what the drug did to people?" he asked, rubbing his chin.

"Son, you may find this hard to believe, but I don't believe that your father ever realized what he was doing or how the drug would affect anyone. All that mattered to him was the power that money gave him. It wasn't until after he met me that he realized that he could be liked and respected even if he didn't have money."

"He really was going to leave everything for us, Mom?"

"Yes he was, son. I believe that your father was happy for the first time in his life, and money was less important to him. He had begun investing in legitimate businesses shortly before was arrested. He was buying antique cars and having them reconditioned, and was doing legitimate business with Japanese business-men, but then he was arrested and the chance to change his life never came."

"Weren't you angry at my dad for deceiving you?" His voice was almost a whisper.

"I was discouraged with him at first, but I couldn't be angry at your dad. He was already paying for everything he had done and so much more. There's something that you don't know about your dad, son, that I think you'd like to know."

"What's that, Mom?"

"Your dad is very talented as an artist. God gave him a genuine gift, but he never knew how to take advantage of it, and his parents didn't pay any attention to it or offer him any support, so he never pursued it when he was younger. When he was in high school he won a contest for a drawing he made. His art teacher told him many times that he had a gift and that he should take advantage of it. He really believed in him and gave him a lot of support. He admired and respected your dad because of his talent and because he was a good kid."

"That's a shame that his parents didn't recognize his talent or support him."

"Yes it is, son, but you know, when I last saw your father, he told me a story that I don't believe he had shared with anyone else. When he was in school, he really liked and respected his art teacher, and he wanted to make him proud and show him that someday he would be someone important. Many years later, when your father had built his enterprise, he had bought himself a brand new Mercedes. He was sitting at a red light when a car pulled up next to him, and there was his art teacher. He glanced at your dad and waved hello, but your dad could see discouragement in his expression, because he knew where the money came from to buy that Mercedes."

"Did he talk to his teacher, Mom?"

"No he didn't, because he was at a stoplight, but you know what your dad said to me that was really sad? He said that as he made eye contact with his teacher, he felt superior, and looked at his teacher with arrogance, as if he were saying "See what I'm driving?"

"How old was he, Mom?"

"I believe he was about 23 years old then, but what your father also told me about that story is that when he was alone later that day, he felt the shame that he couldn't hide from himself. He said that he realized that what he had understood about life wasn't really true at all. He said he was never going to forget the way his teacher had looked at him, and he felt sad that the respect and admiration that his teacher had once had for him had been replaced with shame and discouragement."

"I'm glad that he somehow still had some shame, but it's sad that his love for money was bigger and more important than anything else in life," Joel said, wrinkling his nose.

"Yes, I agree. Son, would you like to meet your father's family?" she asked, cupping her left elbow with her right hand, as she tapped her lips with her fingers.

"Where are they, Mom?"

"They all live in Chicago. His whole family got out of the business, and they all have families and regular jobs like normal people. They've been wanting to meet you for a long time."

"Have you been in contact with them all these years?"

"No son, I haven't. I actually wanted nothing to do with your dad's family after he was arrested. Last year when I was ill, your aunt called me. Even though I had stayed away from them, they always somehow looked out for both of us. She wanted to show her support during my treatments and we speak often, but I told her that you didn't know anything about your dad, and that I would share your father's secret with you on your 18th birthday, and then it would be up to you whether you would like to meet them or not."

"Let's see how everything goes with Dad, okay Mom?"

"I'll respect your decision, son. I just want you to know that your father's family is no longer involved in anything illegal."

"What about my grandfather; is he still around?"

"Your grandfather passed away recently, and he never got the chance to talk to your father again to make amends. Your aunt tells me that unfortunately your grandfather died an ignorant man, since he still loved money more than he ever loved his family and never apologized to any of them for their upbringing."

"That's a shame, Mom."

"Son, your father told me that when they were young, all his siblings were hardworking and would have been very successful at anything they tried to do, but unfortunately your grandfather gave them the wrong foundation. But one thing is very clear to me, son, and that's that your father loved his mother and all his siblings with all his heart, and they all loved him, especially his little brother."

"Have they visited my dad?"

"Only your aunt and your grandmother have visited him. His brothers may never see your dad again, because of their involvement in the business. Four of them served different short terms in prison, but they can never visit him. I know that if any of them could go back and change their life, they would all choose a different lifestyle."

"I'm glad to hear that Mom. I really believe that we are the result of our upbringing and our circumstances, and I can see how my grandfather influenced his family the wrong way. At least they all went on with their lives, and

I'm truly happy for them. Thanks for the great conversation, Mom, but we're coming into Canyon City now," he said as he gently tapped the brakes and slowed down.

"I'm glad we had this conversation, son. It will prepare us to meet your dad tomorrow morning." She spoke softly, thinking about how generous and kind her husband had always been and how he had truly sacrificed his life for his loved ones.

As Joel pulled into the Best Western parking lot, he realized that the next day was going to be one of the most important days of his life. He pictured his father sitting in his cell at that moment and hoped that one day he would have the opportunity to spend some time with him and show him how beautiful life was, even if they didn't have a lot of money.

He smiled at the beautiful sight of the moon resting in the evening sky among the bright stars. He got out of the car and looked at the sky, feeling collected and tranquil. It felt like his heart was as serene as the sky. The next day would be unforgettable, and he prayed that one day he would have the good fortune to share the magic of looking at the moonlight with his father.

Eighteen

$H$is mother got up early and was ready to go have breakfast before they drove down to the prison. Their night at the hotel had been pleasant, since the staff was very nice and friendly.

She waited for Joel to finish showering, and when they were both dressed and ready to go, she asked him to say a prayer together before they left the room. Joel gladly obliged.

The hotel offered a complimentary breakfast, but in front of the hotel was an IHOP and right next to it was a Chili's restaurant. They opted to walk to IHOP and have a meal, since they would be inside the prison the entire day.

As they stepped outside the hotel, they were both wearing jackets and the sun filtered through the clouds, signaling the end of the morning rain. The wind was sighing and lashing the treetops, and the branches moaned.

They went inside the restaurant. It was only 6:00 a.m. and they had just opened. There were very few patrons that early in the morning. Their waitress was very friendly and quickly took their order and brought their meals.

As they ate breakfast, neither of them could contain their joy. Visitors would be allowed after 8:00 in the morning, so they decided that they would leave around 7:15 a.m., since the prison was less than 20 minutes away.

They enjoyed breakfast, and once they left the restaurant, they were ready to drive from Canyon City to Florence. According to the GPS, it would take them 17 minutes to get there.

Perhaps it was because they were both so excited about their visit, but they rode in silence until they entered Florence. Joel didn't really know much about Colorado, but he was shocked as he drove into Florence. It looked almost like a ghost town. Somewhere in town a dog howled, a fitting sound of pure desolation. The town was out of place among the rolling hills of yellowing grass. The old road was barely visible through the vegetation growing over it, and the dilapidated buildings that had once stood out on the main street had the feel of a movie set. Some of the homes had windows that had shattered because of weakened structures and rotting boards. Some were broken, and others were barely hanging in some of the abandoned homes.

He encountered very few cars as he drove into town toward the road that would take them to the prison. He could see that weeds were decorating the cracking asphalt on the lonely roads. The environment was so different than in Canyon City just a few miles away.

As he drove in silence he couldn't help but wonder what sort of lives the residents of that town led. He was very fortunate to have grown up and be living in one of the most beautiful cities in the country.

He slowed down when he realized they were approaching the entrance of the prison and made a left turn, not paying attention to the sign that was posted right at the entrance. He slowed down and drove toward the gated entrance. A uniformed female prison guard approached the vehicle.

Joel rolled the window down and said, "Good morning; this is our first time here. We're here to visit my father, and I'm not sure if I'm in the right place."

"Visiting hours start at 8:00 in the morning. You have to go around here and make a U-turn, and you need to park behind that vehicle that's parked on the side of the road. They're here to visit an inmate as well. We will open the gate promptly at 8:00 a.m., and you'll follow that car once we have opened," she said in a friendly tone.

Joel slowly made a U-turn and parked directly behind the SUV that was waiting along the side of the road. A few minutes later the white SUV in front of him pulled up to the gate. He slowly followed it.

As he approached the gate, the same prison guard met him. "Good morning. I will need both of your IDs," she said as she walked around the vehicle and wrote down what Joel assumed was the car's make, model and license plate number. His mom took her ID out of her purse and handed it to Joel to give to the prison guard, and Joel had taken his ID out of his wallet as well.

"Who are you visiting today?" she asked as she came back to speak with Joel.

"We are here to visit Daniel Conti. He's in the ADX prison building," he answered as he handed her the IDs.

"Are either of you carrying firearms, any type of weapon or any form of illegal drugs with you or inside the vehicle?"

"No ma'am, we are not," Joel responded. He expected that they would be asked to exit the vehicle so she could search them, but they were not.

"You will take this road all the way to the end, and you will see the ADX building on the left side. You will go inside the building and let the guard there know that you're here for a visit."

"Yes, and thank you, ma'am," Joel replied as he got the IDs back from the prison guard and slowly accelerated toward the road that she had pointed out.

Everything was exactly as he had read about the facility. They parked the vehicle and walked slowly into the building. At the front desk sat a male prison guard who greeted them, saying good morning.

Joel's mom told him that they were there to visit Daniel Conti, and they were asked to sit down and wait for a few minutes as he completed a task. Two very contemporary black leather couches adorned the waiting area at the entrance. As they took a seat, they realized there was no one else visiting any inmates.

A young white man was mopping the floors, keeping to himself, but managed to smile at them when they looked his way. The prison guard then asked them to come back up to the counter so that he could check them in. Because that was their first time there, they had to have their pictures taken and printed.

They had to sign in in a register book, print and sign their names, and write the name of the inmate and his registration number so that they could get him ready for their visit. There were two bathrooms available for public use. You couldn't lock the bathroom door. There was a sign on the door that you had to slide from one side to the other to show that the bathroom was either occupied or vacant.

His mother asked if she could use the bathroom and Joel waited for her to come out. Once she was out, the prison guard gave them each a locker key so that they could place all of their personal items, including their jackets, inside the locker. Their cell phones would have to stay inside the vehicle, so Joel had to run outside to the car to put their cell phones inside the glove compartment, then come back inside.

After they put their belongings inside the locker, they had to walk under a metal detector to ensure they weren't bringing in any metal items. His mother had to take off her boots because they had a silver buckle that triggered an alarm as she walked under the metal detector.

The prison guard commented that the metal detectors were far more sensitive and advanced than the ones used at airports. They were, after all, inside one of the most dangerous federal prisons in the country.

They both went through the metal detector and the prison guard had to stamp their right hands and perform a swab test on each of them. He instructed them to put their palms forward, and they both did. The purpose of swabbing a visitor's hands before they entered the prison was to test for traces of explosives.

This was also now a normal random practice that all airports had in place to ensure that passengers showed no traces of explosives.

A second prison guard had come to the front desk, and he escorted them inside. They first went through a metal sliding door that led them down a set of stairs. At the bottom of the stairs was a huge window that housed another prison guard, who asked them both to place their hands under a lamp to confirm their stamps. The guard behind the window exchanged a radio and a set of keys for the copies of the photos they had just taken with the other guard who was escorting them.

They opened another door that led them to a long corridor with beautiful clean white floors and walls adorned with large carved pictures, attractively hung. Each picture bore a different word. Joel couldn't believe that inside a maximum security prison he would find messages on wooden pictures that read: teamwork, trust, collaboration, integrity, dignity and so many others.

The prison guard stopped almost halfway through the hallway and unlocked a heavy metal door that led them into a big room. As they walked inside Joel could see that immediately to the right, elevated on a platform, were three bathrooms, one for males, another for females and the last one for the staff. Next to the bathroom was a vending machine and a soda/water machine. Directly in front in the same elevated platform were four black chairs attached to the floor, and in front of the chairs were some small children's toys and a plastic children's picnic table.

As you stepped down in front of the bathroom, there was a door that read "Staff only," and to the left were four doors that were closed, and Joel had no idea what they were for. To the left of the vending machines were six phone booths, each one numbered, with a chair for each booth.

They were the only visitors in the room. The guard looked at them and said, "You will be in booth number one." That was the first booth and the most private one, but there was no one else in there. That was all the privacy they were going to get, since their conversation would be listened to and recorded.

Joel's heart was beating very fast, because the moment he had been waiting for was finally there. He followed his mother as they walked towards booth number 1.

Nineteen

Of all the indignities and cruelties that a human being could be subjected to, this had to be the worst. There are so many different ways to torture a human being by inflicting physical and physiological pain, but what Joel was experiencing at that moment just tore into his heart. The pain was overwhelming, and he wanted to know how it was possible that men had the power to control so much in other men.

He was standing directly behind his mother, who was seated holding the phone receiver in her hand, facing her husband through a window for the first time in almost 18 years. How could men prevent other men from demonstrating love and affection through physical contact? Joel could see from his mother's expression that she would have given her life to hold her husband and be held by him, but she could only look at him and smile.

This had to be the cruelest means of punishment. How could men impose such pain on other human beings? Did they not understand that people were not meant to be put in cages, treated as animals or even worse? How could they prevent them from having contact with their loved ones, even just for a few minutes?

Most men inside that prison were serving life sentences in isolation. How could they prevent them from at least holding a loved one, experiencing their contact, if only for a few minutes? Joel could see that his mother, although she was smiling, felt the inner pain of not being able to hold her husband.

Why didn't they think of the loved ones? They had done nothing wrong, yet they had to endure the pain of needing and desiring to hold a loved one, to have some sort of contact with them, but not being allowed to. How many mothers, fathers, brothers, sisters, sons, daughters, husbands, and wives had stared through that same glass, feeling nostalgia, sadness, denial, anger, and often desperation?

He looked at his father for the first time in his life. He had jet black hair with shades of gray, and bristly eyebrows. His hawkish nose and defined cheekbones sat above a concrete jaw. His Titan shoulders were part of his burly physique. He smiled at him, and his sea rover-blue eyes twinkled. They were round and shone as bright as the evening stars when they were alight with joy. He could not hear what he was saying as he spoke with his mother while looking at both of them.

His mother had asked Joel several times if she looked old. Joel would only laugh and respectfully joke with her about her appearance. She told him that she wanted her husband to still find her attractive. Joel told her that she was strikingly beautiful, and that even a blind man could see that, and that he was sure his father would find her as beautiful as the last time he had seen her.

She wore vibrant clothes in a non-conforming way. She was wearing simple black dress slacks with a deep blue sweater and a multicolored scarf wrapped around her neck.

Her beautiful black hair had grown out again, and it plunged over her shoulders. She had a shapely, twine-thin figure. Her waist was small and she had a polished complexion. Her arched eyebrows looked down on sweeping eyelashes, and her enticing green eyes gazed at her father. When she smiled, her halo-white teeth lit up the room. Her smile could jolt you like an electric current when she gave you her full attention. Her voice was soothing as she spoke.

Joel was almost in a trance as he watched the way his parents looked at each other. He could see that they still loved each other as much, if not more, than when they had last seen each other. How could that be possible? Could human beings really experience that kind of feeling for one another for such a long time with no contact? He could only hope that one day he would meet someone that he could share that kind of love with.

His mother was smiling and giggling like a teenager, and he could see that his father could not take his eyes off of her. She was so happy to see him, but he knew that she yearned for his contact, if only to hold his hand, but that was not going to happen.

"I'm doing great!" she said with a smile that could not be contained.

"Yes, I'm feeling so much better, and I'm almost back to being myself again."

"Of course I've missed you. There wasn't a single day that I didn't think of you and miss you," she said with wide, glowing eyes.

"I can't believe that I'm really looking at you, Daniel. In spite of everything, you look wonderful."

Although Joel could not hear what his father was saying, he could see that they were both talking over one another, babbling. They were both laughing like children, so full of joy and contentment. They were not using the speaker phone.

"Yes, it's so wonderful to see you, Daniel. I've been dreaming of this day for so many years. I want you to meet Joel and talk to him," she said as she turned and gestured to Joel to come sit where she was and take the phone.

"I'll have him talk to you, and then you and I can talk again. Yes, I love you too, Daniel," she said as she handed the phone receiver to Joel. She was crying when she turned and faced him. Tears rolled down her cheeks as she looked at Joel.

Joel rubbed his hands down one pant leg as he sat where his mother had been sitting. His hands were shaking, and he cleared his throat before he spoke.

"Hi Dad, how are you?" His eyes were soft and filled with an inner glow.

"I've never been better in my life, son. I'm so happy to finally meet you." He had a volcanic voice, full of vigor.

"I'm so happy to finally meet you as well," Joel responded, with a smile that lit up his face.

"Well you've certainly grown quite a bit since the last time I saw you, Joel," his father said, his voice filled with emotion and happy tears rolling down his shining cheeks. "The last time I saw you, you were lying on my stomach. I think you've definitely grown a few inches." He smiled, showing his laugh lines.

"Yeah, I would have to say I have grown a few inches, Dad, since you last saw me." His voice was full of emotion as he witnessed his father crying.

"You're everything that I hoped you would be, Joel. I'm so proud of you, but I'm even more proud of your mother."

"Thanks, Dad. My mom is just an amazing human being."

"I know what you mean, son. She's a very special woman, and we are both very blessed that she came into our lives."

"I know that, Dad. Every day that I see her and spend time with her, I realize that. I'm so glad that I'm here meeting you and talking to you. There are so many things I'd like to ask you."

"You can ask me whatever you'd like, son, but when you first wrote me back, Joel, you asked a very important question. You asked if in my environment I had ever met any men that had inspired me, and what qualities they possessed that led me to look up to them. I didn't answer your question in my last letter because I wanted to meet you and give you an answer in person."

"Why in person, Dad?"

"Because I wanted to look at you when I answered that question. I want you to see me when I give you my answer, and for you to see my sincerity. Most people believe that men and women who are in prison have a stigma; that we lack morals, principles, and integrity, and that we are all bad and evil, but that's not the case, son."

"I don't believe that, Dad," Joel responded as he pushed his shoulders back.

"I'm glad to hear that, son, but as I look at you right now, I want you to know that I've met many great men in prison. What inspires me about them is that they will always say what is right, not what is easy. They're men who carry themselves the same way, regardless of whether they're surrounded by their friends or their enemies, men who despite of their misfortunes try to find ways to better themselves every day, men who keep their word and are consistent with what they say, men who understand the true meaning of integrity, or my meaning, which is doing the right thing when no one is looking, men who have power over others, but don't take advantage of that, men who don't speak ill of others, including their enemies, unless it's to their face." Daniel spoke boisterously, tilting his head back.

"Are you one of those men, Dad?" Joel asked softly.

"What do you think Joel? Do you think your old man is the kind of man that I just described?" Daniel said as he closed his eyes and sighed.

"Of course you are one of those men, Dad. There's no doubt about that, because that's exactly how I was raised, and it was from you that we learned so much," Joel answered with a gleam in his eyes and a satisfied smile.

"Thank you Joel, for believing in me." His cheekbones rose with a prominent smile.

"Have you ever had any men in prison tell you that they admire you? Do you think that you've inspired other men to see life as you do, Dad, and to think like you?" Joel asked as he made direct eye contact.

"I have to tell you, Joel, that I've met many men in prison that I regard as friends, and many times they have spoken well on my behalf and told me that they admire the man that I am, and the feeling of knowing that they respect and admire me is great, but son, let me tell you that there's no greater feeling than when a foe speaks well of you. That's when you know what you're truly worth," Daniel said as he took a deep breath.

"I'm so glad that you're not only the way I hoped you would be, but even more admirable than I could truly know, Dad."

"What do you mean, son?"

"At first, I had my doubts and reservations about you, but now I know that everything Mom said about you was true. I'm sorry that you've been in prison so many years," he said as his green eyes narrowed and his eyebrows furrowed in concentration. "I wish things had been different for you, for all of us."

"I know what you mean, son, but I did commit a crime and I should accept my punishment and see it as one of my life's greatest lessons. I accept that I am the man I am today because of the mistakes I've made and the lessons I've taken away from each of my mistakes," he said, letting out a huge breath. "I don't live my life with any regrets. I just focus on today and doing things today that will enhance my tomorrow."

"You're so right, Dad," Joel said with a slow smile.

"I have to tell you, son, that as selfish as this may sound, I don't regret anything about my life. I wouldn't change a single thing in my life, because if I changed anything, it would change everything I am today, and I don't care to be anyone else but who I am today and who I want to be. I know that what I say may sound selfish, but I can assure you, son, that I'm far from that. I always kept you and your mother in my mind. I'm even okay with my life sentence, which I disagree with, and in a weird way, I'm grateful for it," Daniel said, crossing his arms as he smiled.

"I understand what you mean, Dad, but I still hope that one day you'll be released from prison. Then you can share so much more with me about life, and I can master all of the principles in every missive you wrote for me," he said, maintaining eye contact with his father.

"Joel, how did you really feel about receiving all my missives?"

"Well it was a huge shock for me at first, Dad. I didn't know anything about you, and I'd never really questioned Mom about what had happened between you and her. I wasn't sure; I felt a bit confused and surprised, but after reading your letters over and over and having long conversations with Mom, everything made more sense to me, Dad."

"Do you feel that my missives helped with your upbringing?" he asked, leaning forward toward the glass.

"Yes, of course I do, Dad. Since I got your missives I've had time to talk to Mom about you and how she felt about receiving your missives herself. I'm sure that she'll tell you herself, but she really believes that it's thanks to those missives that she was able to get through life and be more prepared to confront anything that life threw her way, including her most recent medical condition," Joel said, putting his hand on his chest.

"I'm so glad to hear that, son. You have no idea how many times I had to go back and rewrite each missive. Remember, I had an entire year to complete each missive, and many times I had to go back and change or add something to each missive. I can't tell you how many times I rewrote each missive. I wanted to make sure that my messages would help you understand things better and inspire you to be the man that you are today."

"I'm so glad that you did that for Mom and for me. I feel so much more prepared to take on whatever life challenges may come my way, but I've also learned to give priority to the things that truly matter and stay away from the nonsense."

"I'm so glad to hear that, Joel. Listen, I have great news for you and your mom. In the last letter that I mailed you, I mentioned that I submitted an application to see if I would qualify for a sentence reduction, and I received notification that my request is under review. I have never given up, son, and I never will." He spoke with his chin held high, his neck exposed as he inhaled deeply through his nose, exhaling through his mouth.

"That's wonderful news, Dad!" As Joel turned around and told his mother what her father had just told him, she smiled and covered her mouth as she said, "God is great."

"I know that I'm going to be a free man soon, son. I've already paid society for what I've done, and I'm ready to come back and restart my life again. How would you feel about letting me back into your life?" he asked, raising his eyebrows and offering a questioning gaze.

"I'd love to have you in my life, Dad," Joel responded, locking eyes with his father.

"How about your mom? Do you think that she'd let me come back into her life?" he asked, parting his lips slightly.

"You'd have to ask her that, Dad, but knowing her, I know that she'd love to have you in her life as well. You know that she never dated anyone ever, Dad. She's always loved you and only wants to be with you, but that conversation is one that you need to have with her. Mom is such an admirable woman," he said with a very satisfied smile

"Yes, of course, son. I'll have that conversation with her, but you know, son, I always knew that she was a great woman, but I never realized that she would be the woman that she is: a warrior, a fighter, but still always a lady."

"Yes, she's pretty unique, Dad. We're both very blessed that she's part of our lives."

"You're so right, Joel. Son, of all the missives I sent you, which one was the easiest for you to learn and adapt to?"

"Most of them were very adaptable, but the easiest one for me was to "laugh more." I truly believe that laughing as much as Mom and I have in our lives is what got us through all of the hard times."

"That's great, son. Laughter should always be part of your life, every day. You can't lead a life without laughter, no matter what your circumstances are. I laugh as much as I can. I read books that make laugh and feel good about myself. I think back to my childhood memories, when I was really happy and laughed a lot."

"That's wonderful, Dad."

"What was the most difficult of my missives for you to understand and adapt to?"

"That would be "don't worry about things you can't control." When Mom first got sick, I was really worried about her, and I kept thinking about everything that was happening. The worst thing was that in my mind I was thinking about everything that could go wrong."

"So how did you overcome that, son?"

"It was Mom that helped me get through it. She never worried about anything, and she would get a little upset with me if she knew that I was worried. She always stayed peaceful inside, and she shared that with me. Her faith in God is huge, and she focused only on what she could control."

"Son, I understand that as young as you are, it must have been very hard for you to endure."

"It really was, Dad, but Mom was always there to remind me that I had nothing to be worried about; that I had to put my faith in God's hands."

"Yes, God is everything, son, and your faith is what will get you through anything in life."

"I'm so glad that even though I wasn't there I was able to be there for you and your mom, son. I want to ask you to do something with me before you and your mom leave today."

"Sure, Dad. What can we do for you?"

"I want us to pray together and give our God thanks for allowing us to live and experience this wonderful moment, and ask him to let us experience even more joyful moments as a family. What do you say, son?" he asked, sitting stock-still.

"Of course we can pray together, Dad," Joel responded, as he turned toward his mother again and asked her to come closer to him and his father.

Most people would think that God would never find a home inside a maximum security prison, but God was there right that moment as Joel, Daniel and Alexia prayed as a family for the first time. The faith that they shared brought them closer as a family and as children of God.

Joel handed his mother the phone receiver and held her hand as she bowed, closed her eyes and leaned in toward the glass. She gently bit her lip, and with a trembling voice began praying aloud. Joel felt a floating sensation, as if all of his burdens had been lifted, and then a jolt through his body.

"Dear God, we are gathered here as a family for the first time in so many years, and for that, dear Father, we thank you. With humility we come to you to ask that you forgive all our sins and wrongdoings. Today we thank you not only for allowing us to share this miraculous moment, but also for life itself, our health, our family, and all the wonderful blessings that you give us, dear Father, that perhaps we do not deserve. We beg you, dear Father, that on this day you give us the wisdom and the strength to continue to be the best that we can be; to be an image of you. We ask that you help each of us to become an instrument of your peace and that today you bless every single person inside this prison and give Daniel, dear Father, the opportunity to be released from this prison soon. Bless him and bless our family, dear Lord, and don't forget those who are ill, suffering and less fortunate; bless them all, dear Father. Don't forget, dear Father, to send your blessings to all those men and women who have power and control over religion, politics, the home, the schools, and the workplaces, whose minds and hearts are filled with anger, greed, resentment, frustration, and hatred. We pray that you reach into their minds and their hearts. Fill them with love, patience, kindness, and hope, so that they can help instead of hurt other people in this world. We ask for all these blessing in the name Jesus Christ your son, dear Father, and we beg that you have mercy on all of us and lead us away from any temptation and only onto the path of righteousness. Amen."

Daniel and Joel echoed her as they both said, "Amen."

"Thank you for praying the way that you did for the world, darling." Daniel said with a gleam in his eyes.

"Thanks for letting me pray for all of us," she responded with a warm smile, as she remembered how her husband had always called her "darling" when they had first met.

They continued talking for hours, and every word that was said was magical, full of hope and love. As each hour ended, they would have to hang up the phone, and Daniel would have to call them again, and the clock would reset for 60 minutes.

They all felt very blessed, with God's presence in their hearts and minds. It seemed that the hours had flown by, when they were told that visiting hours were coming to an end. They had so much more to talk about and so much to share, but they were all walking away with so much joy and gratitude in their hearts.

Joel said to his father, "We'll be back again tomorrow to visit you. Take care of yourself and remember that we love you." He sat up straight, very focused.

Daniel put his hand on the glass, and his son put his hand up to meet it, as if they were going to press their hands together. They both yearned for that human contact as father and son, but knew that it would not happen that day.

"Yes, son, I will see you tomorrow, God willing, and I love you both more than you can ever imagine. Please take good care of your beautiful mother for me," he said, clearing his throat.

"Visiting hours are over," the prison guard announced.

"Of course I will, Dad." Joel put the phone back on the receiver and got up from the chair. He watched as his father got up and put his hands behind his back. He squatted a bit as he leaned against the door to have the guards put handcuffs on him before they opened the door and placed shackles around his feet and chains on his waist.

Joel felt a bit tense in his stomach as he watched his father. Then he saw his mother's sparkling eyes and weightless gaze, and heard her sigh with satisfaction and say in a very caring, warm voice, "This too shall pass, Joel." She reached out and took Joel's hand.

He had thought that his mother was going to break down and cry as she witnessed her husband being handcuffed and escorted out like a common criminal, but she maintained the same control as always. He wasn't sure why he had thought that she would react differently.

She was in every sense of the word a true warrior. Life had challenged her faith and her strength, time after time, and although she had fallen and hit bottom, she always got up, never giving up. His mother was a perfect example of what God wanted all his children to be. He loved and respected her so much. He thought about the last time she had looked into his eyes the way she had just then and uttered the same words, "This too shall pass, Joel." It had been the last time she went into surgery. She had been right; it had all passed.

She had told him once that everything in life passes, that nothing lasts forever, and that even pain is temporary. Any type of pain will eventually fade and no longer exist. Joel understood that although he was so grateful to God for giving him the opportunity to meet his father and have such a wonderful conversation with him, he still could not avoid feeling pain in his heart, because now he really understood where his father was.

They went through the same process as before to leave the visiting room and go back upstairs to the front desk. They removed their personal items from the lockers and returned the locker keys to the prison guard, and he gave them back their IDs.

Joel took his mother's right arm and wrapped it protectively around his left arm as they walked out of the building that his father called home. He had heard that faith could move mountains. His faith was huge as he escorted his mother outside.

They walked slowly away from the building that housed so many men. Despite their mistakes, many of them were great, noble, kind men who had more integrity, self-respect, and love than those that guarded them.

As Alexia looked back at the building, she realized that God was there at that very moment, blessing her husband and every man inside the building. With each step they took forward, the building slowly became a shadow, turning smaller and smaller. God bless them and keep them safe, she prayed. She kept smiling as she remembered her handsome husband, but also smiled at the idea of who her husband now was. Secretly she thanked God for Daniel, for the man he had become and for so much more.

They drove back in silence to the hotel, and then they talked much more about Daniel the father and Daniel the husband. They were caught up in the moment and the wonderful conversation they were sharing. A few hours later, they left their hotel room and walked over to Chili's to have dinner, since they had not eaten since early that morning.

It was dark as they left the hotel building and walked out into the night.

Joel could see the moon, a ghostly silver disc in the lonely sky. Its beams spilled across the shadow of the mountain like lines of glittering silver fire. It was a deeply moving scene. Sequin-silver stars glistened like beacons of hope for all of the lost suffering souls in the world. It looked as if there were a snowfall sparkling in outer space, and Joel felt so blessed and privileged to witness it.

He took a deep breath, stopped for a second and looked at his mother as he said, "One day I will have the opportunity to share this same sight with my father. Just because I can't share it with him right now, doesn't mean that I never will." He spoke softly, slightly parting his lips.

"Of course you will, son, and don't forget: we learn from yesterday, we live for today, but we always hope for tomorrow, and always remember that better things are coming," she responded, smiling.

"Yes, Mom, you're right. The best is yet to come. You've always told me that God is working things out right now, even if we don't feel it, but we have to keep our faith and be thankful, because where there is faith and where hope grows, miracles will blossom."

"That's right, Joel. I'm so glad that you truly understand that, son," she said, holding her chin high.

"Mom, I think it's time we did what we promised we were going to do. It's time to share and pass on all the wisdom my father has shared with us to the entire world. What do you think, Mom?"

"You know, son, it took your dad a lot of courage to mature and grow into the man that he now is. Today I witnessed that the loneliest people are the kindest, and the people who face challenging circumstances smile the brightest. The most damaged people are the wisest, and all they want is to prevent others from making their same mistakes and suffering the way they have suffered. It's time to share what we know and what we now understand with the whole world."

"Tomorrow we start a new chapter in our life, Mom. We may not be there yet, but we're closer today than we were yesterday. Today we're wishing, but tomorrow we start doing. We will rise by lifting others; our main purpose is to help others, and I truly believe, Mom, that true power lies in the ability to do good for others. We're meant to serve and show compassion and the will to help others." Joel said.

"Yes, son, just as the moon glows like a silver halo in the sky tonight and gives us the miracle of light, we will be the beacon for all those facing darkness in their lives. God will be our guide, and we will bring light to those who are willing to open their eyes, ears, and hearts to us."

Twenty

As they stood on the cliff, they could see a fraction of the white sand, shining like buttery gold. Wands of magical light caressed the languorous sea as the limitless sky gazed down upon the dome of beach. They could see beachgoers lazing along with sun-stained bodies as the waves creased and churned in the sea.

In the distance, streamers of tapered light splayed out, flowing through cracks in the cloud. Arrows of sunlight bathed the ocean, lifting their spirits. They decided to clamber down to the beach.

The waves were rippling onto the feather-soft sand as the spring winds caressed their faces and ruffled their hair. They walked to their favorite part of the beach, where they could enjoy their surroundings and talk.

Joel turned to his mother and said, "I can't believe that I'm going to be 21 in less than a week; the time has flown by. This is going to be by far the very best birthday I've ever had," he said, with an exuberant grin.

"I agree, son. This is going to be your best birthday yet. We're so blessed to be sharing your birthday with your dad," she said as she turned and looked at her husband, who was sitting next to her holding her hand. He turned his gaze from the ocean to her as she spoke, and smiled warmly at her.

"God is great to all of us. I'm so blessed to be sitting here with both of you sharing this moment and experiencing the magic of the ocean. I still can't believe that I'm a free man, that God didn't forget about me and gave me another chance."

"Daniel, it was a long process, but it was worth fighting and waiting for. I'm so happy that today we can celebrate your one-year anniversary as a free man."

"One year ago, Dad, you were released from prison. Do you remember that when we picked you up and flew back to San Diego, you asked that we bring you to the beach, because you wanted to see the ocean? I remember that we were out here a little bit after midnight, and you made us promise that every year on the anniversary of your release we would visit this place. Of course there was a lot of hugging, kissing and crying all the way from Colorado to California," he said, placing his hand on his chest.

"I do remember that day, son. That day is the third-happiest day of my life. That day I was truly a very happy man," he answered, cocking his head to one side.

"What was the second-happiest day of your life?" Joel asked as he leaned towards his father.

"The second-happiest day of my life was the day that you were born. That day, I knew and experienced a joy that was different from anything else I had ever experienced. I knew that you were brought into this world to bless me, son," he responded with a gleam in his eyes.

"What was the happiest day of your life, Daniel?" Alexia asked, joining the conversation.

"The day that I met you. When I first saw you, I knew that my life would never be the same. I truly believe that I fell in love with you at first sight. You stole my heart when you smiled at me. I kept going back to the bank just to see you," he responded as he embraced his wife and planted a kiss on her lips.

"I feel the same way, Daniel. I can tell you that I truly fell in love when I met you, and I knew that my heart would always be yours, and that it was also one of the happiest days of my life," she said as she took a deep breath.

"This year has brought so much change for all of us," Joel said.

"Yes son, it certainly has. Especially for me, because now I've adapted more to being out of prison and interacting again with society, having people around me. I was in isolation for many years and had very little contact with anyone, so it was challenging for me at first to have people around me without feeling a bit on the defensive. What really helped me overcome that, of course, was the idea of starting a family with both of you."

"I do remember, and I know that it was difficult for you at first, Dad, but with our love and support, you got through it, and now you're here with us."

"I still wake up in the middle of the night sometimes, and for a moment I think I'm still in prison, and then I realize that I'm at home with both of you, sharing a bed with my wife. I'm so grateful to both of you for believing in me and being patient with me this whole year."

"We're family, Daniel. We're here for you and we'll always be together. You invested a lot of your time in writing your book this year, and we're so proud of your involvement with youth and what you're doing to try to inspire others," Alexia said, looking into her husband's eyes.

"I'm really proud of both of you. Mom, you've done so much with your volunteer work with all the cancer patients and survivors that you meet. The meetings you lead are so inspiring and give so much hope and peace to so many, not only to cancer patients and survivors, but also their loved ones," Joel said.

He turned and looked at his father and said, "Dad, you're also contributing to society like you promised. I really believe that your book is going to help so many people lead healthier lives, mentally, physically and spiritually. They really need to learn about all the principles you shared with me in your missives," Joel said enthusiastically.

"Thank you, Joel. We certainly couldn't have asked for a better son. You're such a wonderful man, and we're very fortunate to call you our son. We all promised that we would give back and help others who were less fortunate than us. God has work for everyone to do, and there's no time to stand around doing nothing. We have so much to do, and we'll continue to help and serve others the way God wants us to," his father said.

"Daniel, tomorrow you'll be speaking in front of more than 2,000 people, sharing your wisdom with them. I know that you're going to do great, and that everyone who that attends your seminar will benefit from being there," said Alexia.

"I'm very excited that I'm being given this opportunity, and I'm humbled by the idea that people feel like they should look up to me and learn from me. We're all equal, and everyone is born to be great, to thrive, to be happy. They just need to make some changes in the way they think, eat, and live. People need to take personal responsibility to make things happen. They need to believe in themselves."

"Dad, do you really think that we all have the ability to achieve anything in life?" Joel asked, clearing his throat.

"The greatest achievements of mankind were made possible by people who questioned what impossible was. It takes courage for people to make things happen, to let go of the things that have hurt them and how they have possibly hurt others. Also, you have to show yourself that what's in front of you is more important than anything that's behind you. If you don't learn to forgive yourself or others, you'll never be able to move forward to thrive, and you'll really suffer," Daniel said in a relaxed tone.

"Why do you think that people don't understand such a simple concept, Daniel?" Alexia said, her lips slightly parted.

"Men simply don't really think, darling, or rather, they don't think about the things that matter. They continue to live in their past and feel bitterness and resentment in their minds and hearts. Sometimes your past determines how fiercely you fight for the things that matter in the present and will affect the future. People are often too concerned about what people will think or say about them, but what they should be concerned about is what they think about themselves. That's all that matters," he said vehemently.

"That's really sad, Daniel. I've met so many people who have so much potential, but they're so insecure about themselves because of their past, the wrong decisions and mistakes they made, or the way they were hurt by someone close to them, that they're completely blind to the real person they could be if they just thought differently about everything," Alexia said, shaking her head.

"That's true, darling. So many people miss out on so many opportunities in life because of that. They allow what others say about them to discourage them from following their dreams. They don't realize that every day that they wake up they can start all over again, and that if they fall and fail, they need to get up. They need to know that they must never quit; they must have resilience and bounce back up. Everyone feels pain and doubt, but they can't let that stop them."

"You never gave up, Dad," Joel said, raising his chin.

"Son, giving up was never an option for me. I truly had faith that my chance would come, and every day that I woke up inside that prison cell, I woke up with the mentality that I would one day soon walk out of that place, and I prepared myself mentally, emotionally and physically to be ready. A man I met in prison once told me that I was wasting my time with my faith and my beliefs, because I was never going to leave that place, and son, I could have let what he said to me bring me down, but instead his words made me stronger in my beliefs and my faith. Every aspect of life brings you challenges; all humans go through something difficult in life. The down moments are when the growth takes place, son. No matter what you go through, you have to experience it to become who you are; you must allow your pain to push you to your greatness. Life will knock us down, but we can choose to get back up. You'll never truly know yourself until you're challenged by adversity."

"Daniel, that's why people need to hear you speak, and they need to read your book. Because you're living proof that it doesn't matter what happens in life and how badly you hit rock bottom, that if you keep your faith and believe in yourself and keep going, you will succeed," his wife said, looking into his eyes.

"I'd love to inspire everyone to be the very best version of themselves, but so many people think that because they fall, they've failed. That's wrong; true failure only happens when you fall and decide to never get up again. It's not what happens to you that matters; it's how you react to the things that happen to you that really matters. It's our light, not our darkness that most frightens us, because everyone knows that they can shine and is aware of the light inside of them. People have the power to make their lives beautiful; they just need to decide what they want and what they're going to do to achieve their dreams," Daniel said, looking at his wife and Joel.

"I'm so proud of you, Daniel, and I love you so much," Alexia said as she took her husband's hand.

Daniel tightened his grip as he responded, "I love you both more than you can imagine, and I owe you both so much. I want to thank you for suggesting and inspiring me to write this book, which means so much to me and to both of you. I know that as long as we focus on helping others achieve their greatness, God will be pleased with us, and we'll show God our love, devotion and gratitude through our actions. I'm ready for the next chapter in our life, and I'm going to keep sharing all of my love with both of you."

They stood up together and began walking along the beach, Daniel holding Alexia's hand and Joel walking next to his father. It was a miraculous day, and they felt God's grace in their hearts, knowing that they wanted to share the miracle of true living with the world. They slowly walked away from the beach and out into the world that so badly needed them and the message they had to share.

Daniel's book would bring hope to so many, and they would be inspired to lead their lives as God had intended for every human being. He wanted to teach people to learn to lie in the sun and count all of the beautiful things they could count. He wanted to remind them that if they didn't appreciate what they already had, they would never learn to be happy.

As the new day began, they felt ready to help others achieve their greatness. They looked up at the sky, and in silence each of them thanked God for that moment and asked for his blessings on their new journey.

About the Author

Ana Silvia Contreras lives in San Diego, California, with her husband, Raul Garcia, and two children, Juan Carlos Hernandez and Alberto Julian Hernandez. *Missives of Wisdom from an Inmate* was inspired by letters Contreras's first cousin—currently serving a life sentence in a federal maximum-security prison—sent her.

Contreras actively works as a public speaker, offering help to support groups whose members want to find success in all areas of life. In addition to writing and reading, her hobbies include working out, hiking, and running.

36240485R00109

Made in the USA
San Bernardino, CA
17 July 2016